I0688618

Roman's Rules

Roman's Adventures, Book Two

By

Amber Anthony

Copyright © 2019 by Amber Anthony

eBook ISBN: 978-1-3931055-0-3

Paperback ISBN: 978-1-7343822-0-4

Cover Credits

Cover Artist: Kelly Ann Martin, kam.design

DepositPhotos: heyengel, zhuzhu, romancephotos

Editor/Publisher Credits

Professional Editor Services

Published by Amber Anthony

Printed in the United States of America

DEDICATION

This adventure is for those who relish passion *in later years*. To mature lovers finding loving tenderness. *To friendship caught on fire.* To feelings that are deep-burning and unquenchable. To lovers who wish they found each other earlier, *so they could love each other longer.*

To families coming together. We are rooted together, but each of us grows toward our source of light. May we celebrate each other's light.

Happily ever after *is not a fairy tale*, it's a goal.

Acknowledgments

This book is a product of friendship. Sincere thanks to Kathy and David for welcoming me into your city and your lovely home. You shared Aloha, Ha, the Breath of Life, and Pau Hana. I had to leave so I can go back. Mahalo, my friends.

While Nancy and I were polishing this book, we received the news that one of our earliest mentors was in the ICU with a grave prognosis. Being half a continent away and knowing that our being there wouldn't change the forecast we hunkered down and sharpened our pencils. WWDD was our motto. *Thank you for being there for us.*

We are the product of many mentors. When you have the opportunity to be a mentor, please consider the flame you will kindle in another person.

-Rusty

KIRK ROMAN'S RULES

- Never Date a Client.
- Never Date a Co-Worker.
- Every career decision is a personal decision.
- If it feels hinky, it probably is.
- We're suspicious by nature. It keeps us alive.
- Be intentional 24/7 to overcome uncertainty and complacency.

JAX ROMAN'S RULES

- Appearance matters, and when I look the part, I act the part.
- I am what I eat. Cook well, eat well, live well.
- The 'buddy system' keeps us alive.
- Sleep deprivation degrades performance, get proper rest.
- There's a fine line between arrogance and confidence.
- There's a fine line between stupidity and bravery.
- Confidence is king, be decisive.
- Don't make snap decisions.
- Avoid uncertainty or hesitancy.
- I cannot rely on technology.
- I always have something more to give.
- No one is perfect. I seek to know my flaws and improve on them.

PROLOGUE

Thursday, August 13th

Thursday, August 13th

Mackinac Island, Michigan

They held hands and ran toward the ferry dock laughing out loud. The couple escaped the friendly assaults of birdseed thrown by their pursuing wedding guests.

The ferry riders applauded as the handsome man in the dark suit caught up his bride in the linen dress and swooped her over the gap as the ferry chugged at the pier

"Permission to come aboard, sir?" The groom playfully juggled his bride in his arms and saluted.

"Permission granted. We were waiting for you; you didn't have to run." The captain grinned and returned the salute.

The groom dropped his giggling bride's feet to the deck and swept her into a dramatic embrace. "We have a honeymoon to commence, anchors aweigh."

The captain nodded to the deckhands. "Double time, boys, let's get this craft launched."

The bride and groom took the two seats on the starboard rail surrounded by a few full-time islanders.

"Doctor Adams," a small girl ran up and caught the bride's elbow. She grinned shyly at the groom and pointed a wet finger to him. "Is that your husband?"

Kameo knelt to her four-year-old patient. "Yes, Jaxson is my husband as of today."

"You won't be Doctor Adams anymore?"

Kameo looked up at Jax and winked. "No, not anymore..."

****

On the second leg of their honeymoon travels, they prepared to leave Detroit. "More wine?" The flight attendant stood ready to pour.

"After all it took to get here, sure. Then I'll fall asleep."

"Lightweight," Jax teased and offered his glass for a refill. "Yes, please." As the attendant poured, Jax asked, "are we still expecting on-time arrival in Las Vegas?"

"Yes, sir." The man smiled and headed down the aisle to the other first-class travelers.

Kameo studied her new husband, suspiciously. "What have you cooked up, Jax Roman?"

He was the face of feigned innocence. "What? Do you know what it took to wrangle a private plane from Pellston to Detroit in forty-eight hours? I'm just making sure our travel is progressing as expected."

"That's the third time you've asked airline staff if we'll be on time. Either you think you're on a mission or you're planning something."

"I've beat stronger interrogations than this..." He laughed and buckled his seatbelt.

CHAPTER 1

THURSDAY, AUGUST 13TH

LĒʻAHI BEACH PARK, HONOLULU HAWAII

Kirk Roman strolled along the beach at sunrise. When he saw the remains of someone's midnight picnic, he pulled the garbage bag out of his pocket. Wearing rubber gloves and swearing, he cleaned up the mess. *We live in paradise, and we can't pick up our trash.* Peace still painted this tiny public park at six in the morning. A retro desk-style ring tone **shattered** his harmony with nature.

"Roman." Kirk's voice was velvet-edged and as strong as his gym-chiseled physique.

"Romeo! Glad I caught you up!"

Kirk shook his head at hearing his SEAL nickname from his old friend. A wry smile crossed his face as he returned the favor to General Hank Kingston. "Teflon! How'd you get my cell number?" Kirk ran a hand over his sandpaper morning scruff.

"I had to promise dinner to your guard dog at the gym."

Kirk's lips curled upward quizzically. "Which one?"

"Ms. Perry. She said something about being high maintenance, and if I wanted your cell number, I had to tell her a story about you. Romeo, why haven't you staked your claim on that one? I visit, take her out, and all she talks about is you and that sweat factory you call a fitness center."

Kirk's indigo eyes sparkled *Isn't Teflon a little old to still be playing soldier? If the situation hadn't pulled me out of the military, would I still be playing SEAL?* He watched a porpoise breach the water as he walked toward the shoreline, grateful right where he was. "Enough flapping your gums about Jordan." His lips curled in a possessive smile. "What's up, you heading in to take her out *again*? I haven't seen you in a year, and you take *her* out to dinner."

"Romeo, you're not getting any prettier, and I won't be in your neighborhood till January."

"So, this is just a social call?"

"No, I'm calling about your boy, Jax." Every muscle in Kirk's body tightened. "I was in the mess hall, and I turned around and flew back in time thirty years. There you were, kitted out in your gear, that thousand-yard stare in your eye, keeping your men together…"

"So, Jax is in Afghanistan?" Kirk's tension turned to eager anticipation.

"No, had to send him home… the Vice President's press corps got a little too enthusiastic, and someone took a bunch of pictures. Screwed up his covert op."

"Can't say I'm disappointed to hear he's out of the line of fire."

"Don't worry about your boy, Kirk. I get the feeling he's just as capable of taking care of himself as you were."

"That's good to hear." A cloud floated across the sun, and Kirk felt chilled.

"Besides, he's resigned his commission. Didn't you know? He should be out by now…"

Kirk drew a deep breath. "No, we still haven't spoken…" The touches of good humor around his mouth and eyes fell away.

"Wait! Wait! You haven't spoken since we talked about it last year?" Kirk could hear his friend's disappointment over thousands of miles. "I thought I'd convinced you to talk to the boy the last time I was on the island."

"I wanted to; I just don't know what to say…" Kirk admitted.

"Hell, man, you say, Jax, you're my son, I love you, and I want us to get to know each other again. He's become a fine man, Romeo. You're missing out."

"It's not so easy…"

"When did you need it easy? I've never thought of you as a coward, Kirk, don't make me re-evaluate."

The crimson of embarrassment and anger bloomed in Kirk's cheeks. "Are you forgetting what happened the last time I reached out to him? How he told me and all the prison authorities he wanted no communication from me? My sister said he refused to hear my name in his presence."

"That was tough, Kirk, I'll give you that. That was a tough thing to hear from your own kid. But hell, he was what, fifteen, sixteen years old? He didn't know all the facts. His mother just died; his whole life was turned inside out. That was twenty years ago."

"What am I supposed to do, Hank? Insist he sees me if he doesn't want to? I've been hoping he'd come to me."

"When you're in the grave? Be the father here, Kirk. Reach out to your son."

Kirk paused for several seconds and then reluctantly asked, "Can you get me his recent contact numbers?"

****

THURSDAY, AUGUST 13TH

LAS VEGAS, NEVADA

Kameo launched herself through the one-bedroom suite. "Oh, my God, if the ride in the Rolls Royce wasn't enough, the bath is the size of a hot tub, and we have our own steam shower for six!"

Jax buried a grin at her childlike enthusiasm. "We have this two-story suite for three nights. I didn't want jet lag to get in our way. I could cancel the time in Oahu if you like it better here."

Kameo froze. "What?" She seductively ambled over to him

and draped her arms on his shoulders. "I've got you; you've got me. We deserve the best of both worlds."

Jax playfully puckered his lips for a reward. "Kiss me at once, and we'll decide later." His dark eyes held passionate promise.

Kameo danced with the fluffy black bathrobe in the dressing area. "I just want to live in this fuzzy thing…"

Secretively, Jax opened the closet door to see the butler had already unpacked. Two zippered bags from Saks hung behind a bridal white column silhouette evening gown and an equally dramatic ivory cocktail dress. Jax imagined how exquisite his wife would look tonight wearing the classic combination of a demure front with a revealing back. *I wish every crystal on this gown were a diamond. I want her to have only the best. She put her life and career on the line to break me out of prison.*

Kameo ran to join him. "What are you digging into?"

He slammed the closet door and stood guard. "I don't remember you being this nosy before we were married."

She stopped and tapped her finger on her chin. "If my memory serves me correctly, all we had time for in the past was escaping the cops and Phoenix's crew." She gave him a wicked smile, "And a bit of the horizontal mambo."

"If you hadn't had the insight to know that I was innocent, we wouldn't be here today. I'd be dead, and you'd still be a prison psychiatrist." Jax's long strides ate up the space between them. "Right now, it's not about our journey; it's about our destination. Let's journey into that bathtub."

****

Beside the tub, Kameo fanned her fingers under the running faucet, dropped their fluffy black robes, and looked around for Jax.

Jax strode into the marble palace of a bathroom in his boxer briefs and socks. "Hey, you. Did'ja miss me?"

"You… you undressed. Why? That was my job?"

"I sent my suit out to be cleaned. This is what you get." He stood; muscular arms spread wide. Their embrace was juvenile in its exuberance. They ended laughing at arm's length with their fingers interlaced between them. Toddlers would have begun to spin in circles until they were dizzy, yet Jax and Kameo were already dizzy.

Jax started, "Mrs. Roman, we have to get some things accomplished. We need to..."

Kameo was feverish. "Mr. Roman, we need to consummate this marriage. I think our trains are on parallel tracks. Yours is moving faster than mine, but not much faster."

Jax smoothly moved in, hugging her close, inhaling the remnants of the flowers she wore in her thick hair at today's ceremony. She shivered as he pulled the large clips out, and her wealth of hair tumbled around her shoulders. Time stood still as a silent Jax held Kameo close. His lips pressed an intense kiss to her forehead.

"Are you okay, Jax?"

He felt her tremble in his silence. He was aware Kameo was a physician and a psychiatrist to boot. She knew his file front to back before they ever shared the intimacy of a bed. This was her first marriage, but it wasn't Jax's.

Jax purposely lost count of the year Heidi died. They met their junior year of college, they fell in love at Mach speed, and the wedding was two weeks after his graduation. She was Midwest society, and his pedigree was 'iffy'.

Jax and Heidi returned from their weekend honeymoon in the Florida Keys. Jax shipped out, and Heidi dove back into her studies. While Jax fought in post-invasion Iraq, Heidi maintained her Dean's List grade point average.

What if I hadn't gone to Iraq? If I had applied for something stateside, would we have noticed the headaches or paid attention to her nausea? She was alone when the aneurysm hit. She died alone. My wife died alone.

The University of Florida mailed her Doctor of Pharmacy/Master of Public Health diploma to their apartment. It was something Jax couldn't keep. He packed boxes of her mementos, carefully folding the dress she wore when they eloped and mailed them to her relatively unknown parents in New Albany, Ohio. In the same length of time it took for Heidi to pass this earth, Jax applied for SEAL training.

If adversity introduces a man to himself, it also introduced Kameo to Jax. This afternoon, in the arms of his wife, Kameo Alana Roman, Jaxson finally knew who he was.

"Jax, baby?" Kameo's dark eyes sparkled when she spoke his name. "A penny for your thoughts?"

Jax shook out of his flashback and dropped to perch on the edge of the infinity spa tub. Jax pulled her close. "I'm processing being here, married, and unemployed…"

Kameo took his face in both her hands and her brows rose in sweet admiration. "You are married, but remember you provided me with a comfortable safety net. If you want to make tables out of hatch covers on a beach, you can."

Jax's lopsided grin grew wider, and with a definitive nod, his grasp on her softened. "What a virginal white package you are…"

"It's all for you, baby. Do you want to unwrap me?"

Jax ran a slow tongue over his top lip and bit his bottom lip. He steadied himself on the tub ledge. "Uh-huh." He crooked his finger at her. "Come closer, Mrs. Roman. I have work to do." He studied the dress. "Do instructions come with this?"

Kameo giggled evilly. "In case of sexual emergency, pull the cord." Her eyes traveled to the belt of her linen wrap dress and then Jax. "Are you the man who rigged explosives to rescue me? You can't figure out a dress?"

"I don't want to ruin it. But if you don't mind…" He grabbed her by the hips and pulled her closer. She felt his burning attraction. His teeth caught the ribbon at her waist, and he yanked it back.

"Aren't you oral?"

"You're about to find out…" He unwrapped her in a spin, her mahogany hair in a lively swirl. It settled over her luscious lace-covered curves.

"Do you like my wedding outfit?" Her fingertips ran down the ivory lace corset and garter belt.

"Baby, all that lace and those hooks." He caught her between both hands and grinned, palms sliding down the satin slopes of her waist and hips. "Should I leave on these garters? I think I will…" His hand cupped her silk covered mound, and he buried his nose against her.

"Oh, Jax…" She arched into him and sighed.

"Here I am a newly married man, thinking our sex life was going to be the same great sex we've always had and bingo, you raise the ante with this." He shook his head, dark hair falling over his forehead. "I had all sorts of ideas, and all I want to do is throw you on the bed and rip that corset off."

Kameo knelt between his knees. "Perhaps your wife needs to teach you about patience."

"I see where this is going…" His lusty chuckle echoed in the marble room as he stood to let her remove his boxers.

Kameo stepped back and posed her finger on her chin, nodding at his wicked smile. "Lunch on the plane was filling but not satisfying."

I want to stop time and imprint this for eternity. She mused. *He's positively edible with his mussed hair and a five o'clock shadow. Who could resist his washboard abs?*

They caressed, her sighs harmonizing with his deep primal

rumble. Jax whispered, "What kind of satisfaction did you have in mind? Anything in my skillset?"

"Jax, the other night you were… ahh... amazing. There are no words to describe what you did to me. I was so exhausted I couldn't return the favor. Right now, this is your time." His dark eyebrows arched mischievously.

****

Their eyes were inches apart, the better for Jax to see the copper flecks in her ebony depths and the expressive brows framing the windows to her soul. "I've dreamt of this moment, and you feel even better than I remembered." He began the loving task of unlacing her corset. Her silky panties dropped to the floor with the mountain of lace and ribbons.

Now she stood wearing only the sheer garter belt and glistening stockings. She wrapped her arms around his shoulders and straddled his lap. Flesh met flesh. Jax felt Kameo shudder as she balanced there.

He moved to meet her halfway, sitting straighter enhancing connection. Her wealth of hair danced over him, like caressing fingers. She raised her dark locks and twisted them into a knot behind her ear.

"Kiss me, Jax." She presented her ivory neck. Her body flushed as they shared glistening perspiration between them. His kiss caught her, and she giggled. "Jax, take me on a ride."

He was defenseless against her raw charm and sensuality. "I thought you'd never ask." Together they claimed their heaven and slid helplessly into the bubbling tub.

Chapter 2

Kirk and his staff flipped on the lights of Silver SEAL Fitness at O'dark thirty, as usual, to prepare for their seven AM opening. Kirk and his right arm, Jordan Perry, were used to moving by rote at this hour. Somehow, the new instructors seemed to straggle in between 06:35 and 06:55.

He and Jordan, the old-timers, were the first to arrive and the last to leave. Kirk knew why he was the dependable one. He was the owner. He learned discipline at his father's knee. It was honed into him during his naval career and driven home while he was a guest of the state.

Why Jordan was his north star for the past seventeen years, he couldn't say. God knew he didn't pay her enough. Not that she complained about the money.

"How can anyone look this good at this hour? You're not wearing a lick of makeup."

Jordan posed and fluttered her eyelashes. "It's my 'I don't care' routine. If I frighten someone, I don't care."

Her salt and pepper hair bounces and shines in her ponytail. Who said women over 45 shouldn't have long hair? Her hair is gorgeous.

"I use the same routine, but how come you're prettier than me? My old friends take you out to dinner."

Jordan turned on her heel. "Is Kingy coming to the island?"

Kirk dropped the clipboard and straightened his shoulders. "Kingy?"

"You know, Kirk, he knows how to show a girl a good time. He lost Doris about the same time I lost Frank. You can always get a date and join us."

"All you'll hear is war stories if you date Fly Boys and SEALs; you'd be in the middle of our shop talk."

"Speaking of shop talk…" The fifty-something transplant from North Dakota gazed at Kirk over her half-glasses, and her grey eyes sparkled. "I want you to start some new classes." She beamed. "I want to get a pre-natal class started; it's the right time."

"What do you mean the right time? Do you have something to tell me?" Kirk's brows knit as he gestured to her midsection.

"If you're pointing at me, that would be a surprise. However, it's coming into fall, and we've received many requests on the website."

David, the weight training instructor, dragged in looking hungover, drinking a two-liter bottle of water. He smiled hugely at Jordan and nodded to Kirk.

How come I don't get the smile, I'm the boss. Kirk turned back to Jordan and smirked. "Glad I'm not a party animal, but back to those requests. Really?"

Jordan leaned on her elbow at the counter. "Apparently, ladies can't get into Kahuna's classes."

Kirk made a sardonic face. "Big Kahuna Fitness has pre-natal classes?" He shook his head. "What's the liability on that? What if in the middle of class on the count of three, there's suddenly an extra student?"

Jordan shook her head. "You were a Navy SEAL, and you think babies just pop out?" She screwed up her nose. "The worst thing we could have is an unexpected leak. It can't be any worse than the seniors' class."

"It's worse; it's a lot worse. More volume, it's far more slippery. I can't believe I am having a discussion like this before my coffee."

"I guess Kahuna gets the next generation of exercise fans..."

Kirk waved a finger. "Don't go all Kahuna on me.

Jordan shrugged. "The next thing you'll say is we can't have baby massage classes."

"Does Kahuna have that?"

With a shrug of one shoulder, Jordan grinned. "Don't know, want me to call him?"

"Babies cry, they poop and pee and that shit leaks."

"Literally."

"I'll compromise. Put up a questionnaire about prenatal exercise classes while I talk to my insurance man. I do know it's more fun making babies than cleaning up after them."

****

FRIDAY, AUGUST 14TH

LAS VEGAS, NEVADA

The nap was an excellent idea. Jax stood before the bathroom mirror, tying his white silk necktie over a new and freshly pressed dark blue shirt. The lady's maid who took his suit to be cleaned and pressed was now in the other room assisting Kameo into her evening finery.

He gave himself a jaunty smile in the mirror. *She really seemed to like her new dress.* Jax checked his collar and cuffs and went downstairs to view the Las Vegas Strip from his living room window. He poured himself three fingers of tequila and ran the lime around the glass's rim. In the dimly lit room, his reflection stared back at him. His usually clipped military 'do' sprouted small curls at his collar. *Life is changing.*

As he waited for his wife, *my wife,* Jax pondered the irony that the Reposado Tequila he drank was aged in the red clay soil and chiller climate of Mexico's Jalisco Highlands. It was a picturesque area far, far away from Isabel Huerta's Lobos Cartel. The tequila was certainly one of the more pleasant products of Mexico. It was a shame Isabel and her ilk besmirched Mexico's character with her ruthless criminal faction. Jax had reason to know the extent of her ruthlessness. She replaced her lieutenants with alarming frequency. A call to have dinner with the thirty-eight-year-old widow was a crapshoot. A man could end the evening on a slab or kneeling, pledging fealty.

The last man standing, Pollo Phoenix, believed himself to be the victor when he engineered a Senator's death and framed Jax for the murder. Isabel Huerta snatched legal victory from Jax's DEA task force when everyone ended up dead in her yacht's explosion. The explosion heralded the end of the Lobos Cartel, and Jax and Kameo felt they were safe to honeymoon.

He listened to the laughter of the lady's maid upstairs. "Oh, no, Mrs. Roman, you wear the flowers behind your left ear now. It shows you have a husband." Jax snuck to a corner of downstairs where he could watch the women. The maid carefully clipped the cascade of white and yellow plumeria behind Kameo's left ear.

"My dear, you are as lovely as any movie star I have ever dressed." Kameo caught the woman's hand in hers and smiled sweetly. "Our whole staff sends you their best wishes for a very satisfying life."

Once the lady's maid was gone, Jax stood pensively awaiting Kameo's arrival. His breath caught at the sight of her in the glittering long-sleeved dress. They embraced in the glow emanating from the Vegas Strip's throbbing lights. Her lips pressed a light kiss on his jaw. In silence, they watched the colorful discord of light along the strip. Standing behind her, Jax ran a glancing finger down her spine. "I'm glad this dress has no back." That same finger drew aside her long hair, and he kissed her.

"Oh Jax, you keep that up, and we'll be eating cheese crackers and the fruit basket."

"Well, that would blow my plans for tonight."

"I knew you had a secret…"

"As a matter of fact, I do. In all the time we've been together, I never got to show you off. Tonight that changes."

****

The private elevator opened, and Jax escorted Kameo on and nodded to the lift operator. "Private dining, please."

When the doors swooshed open, the maître d' bowed formally. "Good evening, Mr. and Mrs. Roman. It would be my honor to escort you to your dining room. My name is Paul, should you need anything, please ask for me."

Jax nodded. "Good evening, Paul." Jax smiled at Kameo, and they fell into step behind the man. They passed through an elegant, dimly lit lounge with the soft titter of laughter and the rhythm of cocktail shakers. They walked by many patrons enjoying beautifully prepared meals delivered by elegantly dressed servers. Tonight, as his divine wife walked beside him, the room hushed.

I'm going to have to get used to people admiring my wife. I did want to show her off.

The maître d' opened the double doors, and people craned their necks to see this gorgeous couple's destination. Jax allowed Paul to escort Kameo to the table. As Jax drew the double doors closed, his gaze fell on one especially hungry set of eyes, and Jax shook his head and winked at the older gent before closing the doors.

Deep amethyst draperies flanked the tall windows and accentuated the high ceiling. Gilt chandeliers hung with sparkling crystals shooting shards of light about the room. Through the window, they watched the fountains dance.

Kameo folded her hands over her mouth. "Jax, all of this is for us? Look at all the glasses and silverware. Are we going to eat that much?"

"Well, at least a nibble of everything. It's a tasting menu with all the wines." He gestured to sparkling crystal glasses in different shapes and sizes. "But, save some room for dessert, cause it's a humdinger."

"Well, now you've got me intrigued." She looked around and sighed. "Do they validate parking?"

"We don't even have a car, but the Rolls is outside."

Kameo sat as the server pulled out the chair. "You're right; we don't have a car. I married you and don't even know what you drive." *Did Paul just roll his eyes?*

****

Their conversation was low and clever as they shared the sixteen-courses of an unparalleled dining experience. Servers moved intuitively around the honeymooners, anticipating every desire by Jax and Kameo's responses to the chef's artfully presented creations.

They cleared the table for the humdinger of desserts. Kameo left plenty of room for the coconut mousse with lemon cream and pineapple lime compote. Jax anticipated the hazelnut milk chocolate crémeux and praliné ice cream. Paul moved a divider screen to reveal a digital grand piano.

Giggling, again, Kameo shook her head. "No karaoke, please."

Jax wiped his grin away. "No, baby. No karaoke. Someone a lot more talented than me is going to grace us with his brilliant voice." Jax got up from his seat and went to the door. Kameo peeked around to see to whom he was speaking, but her view was blocked.

Jax escorted two elegantly attired men into the room. They proceeded to the piano, and Jax returned to Kameo's side.

"Buona sera, signor e signora Roman. My name is Carlo Luciano, and with your kind permission, I would like to offer congratulations and best wishes on your new life together."

Kameo turned wide eyes to Jax. "*The* Carlo Luciano?"

"Carlo's son and I served together in Iraq." He turned to the famous opera singer and nodded. "Thank you, my friend, for honoring us with your talent."

Kameo listened enraptured as the tenor launched his signature piece. Jax pulled her closer and kissed her ear as they were serenaded. He watched as a tiny happy tear threatened to fall. He caught her hand and kissed her palm. "It's true, baby, we were born to shine, together."

She daintily wiped the demi tear away and nodded. "Every time I closed my eyes, I made a wish, and I believed we'd be together again. And here we are."

Chapter 3

Saturday, August 15th
Las Vegas, Nevada

Desmond Franklin usually enjoyed his job. Stack glasses, connect beer kegs, and stash bottled beer in the coolers. Desmond was tired of dealing with whining bartenders. They pocketed the cash tips on the sly and bitched about sharing the charged tips. *Whiners. What day is it? I need a day off.*

Desmond was one of the handsome young men the bulk of tourists overlooked. He was uncommonly striking in a clean, mother approved manner. He kept fit to make his job more manageable. He swore off drugs and alcohol because his mind demanded it. He didn't flirt with the clientele; he didn't initiate conversations with his co-workers. Desmond *saw* things; he *knew* things; he *felt* things about people.

His broad shoulders tensed at the thought of being on the bar floor. He volunteered to leave and bring back a case of pint glasses. With Desmond's level of 'awareness,' this night was biting into his sanity

"Des, Mr. DeBlasio wants to see you…" Delores pressed the button on the Vitamix, and the end of the sentence was drowned by ice crushed at high RPMs.

****

Desmond slipped into his boss's office. The room was decorated like a luxury auto. Lots of platinum leather and mood lighting. Soft music played from, *where?*

Not tonight, I need my job. Not tonight, please.

Mr. DeBlasio nodded at his arrival, as usual, he didn't make eye contact. "That thing you do, the act you pull when you're bored. You could do that in front of people, right?" The dark-haired man rotated his chair and smoothed back his greying pompadour as he bit his smoking Churchill. "You a magician? You do mind-reading?"

Desmond chewed the inside of his lip. "A mentalist act, you mean?"

"Fact is, the drunk bastard, the amazing asshole couldn't see into his future to know he'd be passed out in his dressing room. He was supposed to do the eleven o'clock show. It's ten-thirty, and we have a full house." Silence, no response from Des. DeBlasio puffed smoke signals in frustration. "I need you to throw on a tuxedo jacket and pull twenty minutes out your ass. Play up to the bald guy with the blonde in the front row, then we'll bring in the dancing girls, and you can go back to tapping kegs."

"Sir, it's not something *I can* pull out of my... ass." Des shook his head, brows knitted.

"Look, Franklin, you're easy on the eyes, go out and make some noise. We'll drop you five hundred. Cash."

That sealed the deal. School loans were due; in fact, he was behind, Des hadn't made his monthly rounds of the small-town casinos to 'win' his usual pot. "Sure, who's the bald man?"

"What? Can't you tell? What kind of a... mentalist are you?"

****

Des debated doing his usual induction, asking the universe for protection and clarity, and then delivering a revelation that would astound and amaze. Then again, he could fake it; he could use the passed-out artist's shill and pocket the five hundred without digging up real dirt.

He ignored the announcer's bombastic introduction. It

wasn't until the broad spotlight hit him, standing down center stage in the musky brocade tuxedo that his spirit guides made the decision for him.

Directly behind the bald man and his blonde 'niece' was a couple straight out of Hollywood's golden age central casting.

The Polynesian woman sat beautifully erect in the clamshell booth. Her ivory gown shimmered, reflecting light around the room. Her dark gaze flitted from left to right, up and down. If her head could swivel like an owl's, *perhaps it would?*

The man in the booth protectively covered her hand with his. He was a machine, with equally dark hair, sapphire eyes, and a deep tan hinting at southern California, not the islands. This man's measured gaze played the other areas of the room as if they worked in tandem from one mind.

The four-piece band played a generic mysterious sounding tune while the announcer asked for silence.

Des approached the recommended couple. The bald man sat satisfied with his young eye candy. They nodded to each other, and Des addressed the blonde.

"Think of a number…." He handed her paper and a pen. "Write it down, hand it to the people behind you." He nodded to the honeymoon couple, yes, they *are* honeymooners. The younger couple looked at the paper and nodded. "Fold it up, sir, hand it back to this gentleman." Gesturing to the bald man, Des returned to their table. The drummer brushed a riff on the cymbals, then silenced the sound.

"Miss, your number is 50."

"50?" The blonde giggled effusively. "Al, he got it, *I picked 50!*" Her date held up the paper to the crowd.

The unseen announcer boomed. "Amazing, let's hear it for Xavier, the Oracle."

Des felt the inextricable pull into his 'zone'. Most women doubled their age; that guess was nothing. *Nada.* He rebuffed his visceral call and paced to the other corner of the stage, stepping down to a Midwestern couple with their adult children.

The mentalist called to the audience. "That was too easy, right?" He nodded to the older man. "Sir, think of a trip you've taken. Think of the person who went with you. What did you do there? Write it down. Share it with the people at the next table." The strangers at the following table silently read "Boundary Waters fishing trip, Eddie, lots of fishing."

The family smiled and nodded, and the woman blocked the paper with her evening bag. "Fold it, fold it again." Des accepted the paper. He ripped it into nothing, dropped it on the table and placed a plate over it. Holding his hands up, Des asked, "Anything left in my hands?" The room shook their heads no. Des bent toward the adult son. "Would you take the paper out of my pocket?" Des held his jacket open, and the man withdrew a heavily taped envelope. "Please, use the knife to open the envelope and read the contents to the room.

The man read, "Boundary Waters fishing trip, Eddie, lots of fishing."

Des turned to the Midwestern father. "Is that what you wrote, sir?"

The older man exclaimed, "Why it is. How do you do that?" The room exploded in cries of astonishment and applause.

Des scanned the room and smiled humbly. The honeymoon couple's aura vibrated at him. Yes, *vibrated at* him. As he headed toward them physically, he walked down his mental staircase of clouds. At 'ten' he opened the door to find himself on a dock. Although aqua waves eventually caressed the shore, they were teeming with disturbing energy. Desmond palmed his face with both hands to veil his reaction to the portent of the message.

The honeymooners moved within new confines, new names. Des saw a sinister woman, property destruction, and a gunshot. Des shook with a vision of the man running to his new bride as the color red encompassed her.

This was not fit after-dinner entertainment. He turned from the couple. Better he should pull people's wedding anniversaries and birthdays. He'd play Sherlock for their pleasure and amazement. Perspiration trailed cold down Desmond's back as the woman's death scene looped in his mind.

Des 'guessed' hometowns and threw out a few Keno numbers disguised as 'your winning numbers'. After twenty minutes of living hell, he bowed deeply when the band struck up the 'mysterious' music. They were some of the most conflicted moments of his life. When he stood erect, the honeymooners were checking their booth and leaving.

I'll catch them at the side door. Des took two steps back, out of the spotlight, and clipped toward the side exit. He hit the door in time to see the man and his wife making their way toward the main hallway.

Excuse me, you don't know me, but your wife is going to be murdered... yeah, that's not a great conversation starter.

"Sir, sir..." Des read the concern on the man's face as his arm encircled the woman's shoulder, and he stepped to shield her. *Protective, good.* "Congratulations on your marriage."

The man tilted his head as his lips dropped at the corners. "Excuse me?"

Des extended a hand, "My name is Desmond Franklin." It squeaked out. "I am a mentalist." *That sounds egotistical.* "No kidding, I really am." The man took his hand, and Des braced himself for the revelation.

Warfare, darkness, bomb blasts, and battleground lamentations.

"Jason Rawling, my wife…"

But you didn't say her name. "Mr. Rawling, if you're concerned about your wife's safety…." The couple shared a look, and then their gazes bore into Des. "Then keep your anonymity. Don't come back to Vegas."

Des's tone became flat, trance-like. His grip on Jax's hand increased, and Des's eyes stayed closed as he whispered, "First Peter, 5:8-11. Keep a cool head. Stay alert. The Devil is poised to pounce and would like nothing better than to catch you napping. Keep your guard up. You're not the only ones plunged into these hard times. The suffering won't last forever." Des felt their handshake burn, and he threw off Jax's hand, stepping back, palms up, physically shocked.

CHAPTER 4

It was a blustery Sunday morning on the island. For a hot second, the weatherman hinted at a hurricane forming. For a change, Kirk made it to the Highway Inn before Jordan. Wearing a plum windbreaker with the hood up, Jordan entered with a serious demeanor, barely sharing a smile with a person she knew at another table. Kirk was about to wave her back when she nodded and slipped out of the light jacket. *She's beautiful in grape or plum or whatever it's called this season. That salt and pepper hair and sunny complexion. Wonder what has her down in the mouth?* "I ordered you a tea, but you look like you could use something stronger."

One corner of her mouth turned up in a smile that didn't quite make it to her eyes. "Thanks, Kirk, you are always thinking of me. I appreciate that."

"From the way you say it sounds like I'm in a small group."

Jordan stretched as she removed her jacket and slid into the booth to wrap both hands around the mug. "You know how some mornings you wake up and you don't quite feel plugged in?"

Silently, the server slid two yogurt and fruit bowls in front of them. Kirk winked thanks and watched Jordan, his chin resting on his clasped hands, his elbows on the table. "It's the wrong day of the month, I guess."

Kirk was flummoxed, women and days of the month were a mystery to him. His brow arched, and he shook his head. "Tell me about it?"

"Today, my sister would have been fifty-one." Jordan stared into the bowl and smashed the colorful fruit into the white yogurt until it was a pastel mash. Then she slid it aside and sipped her tea. "Her daughter had a son a month ago, and of all the people, Andy would have loved being a Granny."

"That's rough, Jordan. I'm sorry…"

"Thanks, you know I don't talk about family stuff much. It never bothered me that Frank and I didn't have kids. My cycles never corresponded with his flight schedule. But I know Andy is bouncing from cloud to cloud watching over that little boy."

"When life feels unfair like this, I remind myself, you are who you are for a reason. I'll bet that little boy will love his Aunt Jordan, and you can help his mother tell him about Andy."

Jordan blinked for a second and then swallowed whatever emotion bubbled up deep inside. "After freezing my ass off in Minot, North Dakota…Frank was stationed there…" She shook her head. "I decided I'd never be cold again, and I moved here." She frowned. "Maybe I should have moved to San Diego to be near Andy and her family.

Kirk's eyes opened wide. "I would have hated that; you wouldn't be here for me now."

She gave him a crooked smile. "I live here for you?"

"It's all a matter of perspective."

Her smile grew genuine. "I do think I've met a nice guy for a change."

"I am a nice guy." Kirk leaned back, his arms along the booth.

"I mean, a man." *I'm a man. Where is this going?* "A man who enjoys boating and travel." Jordan's cheeks blushed as she sipped her tea and spooned fruit to her smiling lips.

"Seriously? That's…" *fucking ridiculous, what kind of answer can I give her that doesn't sound crass?*

"I convinced him to come by the gym when he's on the island."

"Like, work out?" Kirk began chewing more vigorously than yogurt and fruit required.

****

MONDAY, AUGUST 17TH
LAS VEGAS, NEVADA

They boarded the Hawaiian Air flight departing at 1:50 AM. Kameo pulled her hair into a messy bun atop her head as she slid into seat one A. "What do you think that seer meant?"

Jax stood at his seat, his gaze scrutinizing the remaining first-class passengers. In a low baritone, he spoke, his lips barely moving. "He's a mentalist. It's a parlor game." Jax dropped into his seat and planted an undeniably hot kiss on Kameo's open mouth, staunching whatever she would say next. "Couldn't you get used to first-class?" In a sotto vocce tone, he added, "You have twenty million reasons why you can."

"It's more like nineteen, five." She waved her hand in a gesture of balance. "Jax, you didn't sleep right since he said that…. Seriously, Jax, am I going to spend all of it on protection services?"

"Just the interest. I'm pretty sure you already made up that decline. I'm just looking forward to being a kept man."

"You have to be alive to be kept. I have to be alive to keep you." Kameo nestled into his embrace, sneaking a peek at the people getting settled around them. *Let's see who's standing after you meet your dad. Have I overstepped my bounds by locating him?*

In time, Jax and Kameo reclined their seats and held hands all the way to Oahu. She hoped they wouldn't see a billboard with Kirk five stories high. If they did, she might have to distract him with a devouring kiss.

****

HONOLULU, HAWAII

By six-thirty in the morning, Jax slipped a gratuity into the bellman's hands and threw the locks on the suite's double doors.

From where he stood in the foyer, he had a clear sightline through the living room to the patio and on to Diamond Head.

So much for security. What good is a locked front door when the walls facing the pinnacle of all luxurious views on Waikiki were telescoping doors that slid to nothingness? Jax swore under his breath. "So much for the superb sanctity of a stellar view."

They were ensconced in a suite encapsulating unparalleled levels of Aloha hospitality, signed in as Jason and Casey Rawlings. For the next four weeks, they were Honeymooners left to debate devastating comments from a Vegas mentalist.

Nestled in a chaise on the lanai, 'Casey' sat with Gideon's Bible in her lap. "What was that quote, something about keeping up your guard?" She was in that jet lag a mainlander gets when arriving early in the morning on Oahu -- too excited to sleep, too keyed up to absorb the island ambiance. Jax took the Bible from her hands, smoothed back a lock of her hair, and caught the orchid lei with his finger.

"This is a good look for you."

"Salty, don't try to bullshit a psychiatrist."

"Me? Naw, we don't need Gideon to follow us on our honeymoon." He held up the Bible, showing the title page. Her brows knit in confusion. "My buddy back in San Diego? His name is Gideon? Never mind." Jax returned the Bible to a drawer and stretched out with his beloved wife.

"I guess we have lots to learn about each other." She looped her arm through his and played with the leaves on his lei.

"You aren't going to trade me in at the end of this week, are you?" Jax stroked her hip, and it encouraged her to slide her knee over his outstretched legs.

"I am at a definite advantage, having read your file…"

Now Jax grimaced. "At least you can't be surprised at anything I do, right?" He caught her hand and kissed her palm, initiating their first scorching horizontal mambo on their private lanai.

****

TUESDAY, AUGUST 18TH

Kirk took the gym's steps two at a time. He had forty-five minutes to decompress, drink a smoothie, and catch up with Jordan. Sucking on the smoothie, he wondered who sent the four-foot jungle plant. Jordan seemed oblivious as she scrolled through gym business on the computer.

Releasing the fat straw, Kirk pointed to the anthurium. "Did I buy that?"

Jordan bubbled. "Of course, you didn't."

"Good, I didn't think I'd buy anything that suggestive."

Jordan scowled. "What do you mean suggestive? It's a beautiful tropical plant."

"I can't decide if it looks like a baboon's butt or his dick."

Jordan scoffed and pointed her pen at him. "Not everyone has a dirty mind like you. This was sent to me by an admirer."

Kirk's face arranged itself in a sober scowl. "Who?"

"That would be your business because…"

The scowl continued. "Because a nice man would never send a pot of dicks to a lady."

Jordan dismissed him with a wave of her hand. "Kirk Roman, you are impossible."

Kirk rifled through the leaves and stalks looking for a card. "Seriously, this is a lot of coin sitting here. He could have smothered you in roses for what…" he pulled the hidden card from the envelope, "Wade Stieber paid for this." He muttered under his breath. "Would have been a lot more appropriate, too."

"Well, this beautiful plant came with an invitation. I am invited to a new yacht model release party. It's the weekend of August 22nd. I need Saturday and Sunday off. He's promised me a long weekend since I don't work on Mondays."

"That's this weekend; that's pretty short notice."

"I've already checked, and Mona wants the extra hours. You're all covered."

"So, where is this man of mystery?" Kirk leaned against the counter and occasionally nodded as members checked in and left for the locker rooms.

"I have you set up for his orientation tomorrow at one."

"Make sure his medical questionnaire and sign up papers are in the computer." Kirk gave a long draw on what was becoming a tasteless beverage.

"Oh, they'll be there."

****

WEDNESDAY, AUGUST 19TH

Kameo mused as she woke up on the third day of their stay. *I blink, and that magnificent view is still there*. The only difference? The shadows of the clouds changed the colors of the rocky surface hourly. *Same gorgeous weather, every dang day.*

It was magnificent the morning they climbed Diamond Head. As the gate opened at six in the morning, their driver delivered them to the eastern edge of Waikiki's coastline, to the Diamond Head State Monument.

Jax checked his shoelaces before they headed toward the walking path. "The trail to the summit of Lēʻahi was built in 1908 as part of Oʻahu's coastal defense system."

Kameo situated her sunglasses and stared at the summit. "Are we walking all four hundred and seventy-five acres?" Their progress was leisurely as they got to the first worn handrail.

"It'll feel like it. Most of the path is switchbacks. I remember running out here. Of course, I'd wait until most of the tourists were out of my way."

"Of course you would, Jax, you like a special sort of pain, don't you?" Kameo tsked, as a geriatric Asian man jogged up behind them. As he passed, they saw his running jersey already plastered to his lithe frame. "I can see you doing this at his age, while I sleep in a chaise by the pool."

Jax playfully swung his arm around her shoulders. "And I'll bring the grandkids so you can get some extra sleep…"

Kameo startled. "Grandkids? We don't even have kids. How soon?" The thought of dealing with Jax's son or sons was daunting at this point. *What miniature dare-devil hellions would they spawn?*

"Not this week, I thought we'd just dabble for a few months until we get settled…"

"Dabble? Sure…"

Their ascent continued up steep stairs and through a lighted two hundred and twenty-five-foot tunnel to enter the summit. Jax and Kameo punctuated their walk with stops to playfully smooch and point to stand-out homes visible from their altitude.

"This was the station that directed artillery fire from batteries in Waikiki and Fort Ruger outside Diamond Head crater." Jax pointed with his hand. "See the bunkers and the lighthouse?" The stunning panorama postcard view of the shoreline from Koko Head to Wai'anae framed a double rainbow as they were blessed with the misty rain prevalent at that elevation. "We should come back in the winter and watch for humpback whales."

Kameo hung on the worn pipe rail and scoured the neighborhoods below. "I think I want to live on this side. Too bad that lighthouse is occupied."

They leaned back and tried to catch a selfie with both rainbows when an older woman, smitten with Jax, smiled. "May I take your photos? That double rainbow is especially lucky for you two!" Blushing, Kameo handed over her phone, and they posed for the photo. "Now, you have to kiss her under the rainbow." The woman stepped back and began a panorama shot of both rainbows. "Don't move while I catch the whole thing!" The crowd clapped as a few of the pre-teenagers darted squeamish looks at the show of affection. "Now I caught it all. Have a wonderful life, you kids." The woman smiled as she handed back the phone and disappeared into the crowd, descending the metal stairs.

Jax's gaze scoured the changing crowd at the summit. *Is he counting who stayed and who left us?* "So, this is the side where you want to live? Have you picked out a house yet?"

Kameo's hand caught Jax's and brought it to point at the home with the bright red tile roof. "It's like lacquer red, isn't that a gorgeous roof? And the pool... it's built like a lagoon." She brought up photos from a real estate listing. "See, it's almost an acre; we're far enough up the mountain; we'll have a water view..."

Jax caught the phone from her hand and enlarged the photos. "I've been played. I thought I was bringing you up here for a nature hike, and you brought me to look at houses."

Kameo shrugged and grinned. "Tomato, tomahto. It's available for showing this afternoon. I thought after a nice swim and a shower, we could take a look at it."

Jax looked at his watch and nodded. "Better start back now..."

✳✳✳✳

Kirk made a point of being a bird's eye distance from the front desk by twelve-forty-five. Who was trying to romance *his* Jordan? And in he walked, stopping the female conversation at the doors. The women spun in unison to watch him pass through the lobby. *He's nothing that great...* Wade dealt Jordan his most devastating smile. His just-greying hair danced as he threw back his head to laugh at whatever Jordan said. *His teeth look like Chicklets. Are there diamonds embedded in them?* Jordan's gaze swept him in total adoration. She leaned over the counter, and her hand patted his forearm in conversation. *He's not very tall. He's thin, but his face is gaunt. Is he a drinker? I'll bet he smokes.*

Jordan looked around in anticipation. Kirk usually greeted his orientees at the desk. That was his cue to bound into the lobby excited about the new member. He carried a fresh towel, and Silver SEAL water bottle and stood purposefully taller in front of the new guy. Extending the bottle, Kirk opened his mouth to give his usual spiel.

Wade pointed to Kirk's SEAL tattoo. "You were a SEAL. I was a Ranger. Hooah!"

"Around here, it's hoo*yah*." Kirk smiled charmingly. "Let's get you a locker, and we'll get your fitness testing."

Jordan dropped her chin, and Kirk felt her scrutiny every step down the stairs.

Kirk found Wade's level of fitness to be disturbingly equal to his own. *He's ten years younger, though.* Kirk put him on a treadmill and cranked up the angle and the speed. Wade didn't break a sweat. He did focus on his feet.

"Got some foot pain? We've got a great reflexologist on staff."

Wade shook one foot for a second. "These were in my duffle; they aren't my distance trainers. These babies are like concrete." Kirk buried a smile. "You know, Squid, you can amp the speed and crank up the angle, and we'll be here till midnight. I can march as far as you can swim."

Kirk gestured humorously. "That would be very cool, we could make it a fundraiser."

"Sure, if we have fair maidens to give us their favors, you know, like in jousting tournaments? You married, Roman?"

Kirk shook his head.

"You ever date, Ms. Perry?"

Kirk dropped the treadmill angle suddenly, jerking Wade to a stop. "Oh, sorry. No, I don't date my employees."

"Then can you clue me in? Have any idea who's been knocking at her door? Does she have a wild side?"

Kirk ground his jaw. "She doesn't bring her private life into work."

Wade pumped his fist. "That's the kind I like, the sleeper, the ones with a tight lip. They get wild and kinky when you get them unwrapped."

Kirk tossed him a towel and swallowed his irritation. "She asked for this weekend off, said you were making it a three-day thing?"

Wade wiped sweat from his neck and chest with a wicked leer. "Oh, it's a three-day thing. I blog boats, and I picked up a line on a new Dolphin Master Yacht." Wade looked around the room and lowered his voice. "I told her it was a boat party, and that's how it starts. Then Saturday after dinner, I get the keys to a new thirty-five-foot party yacht, for a party of two."

Kirk stood straight, gazing down at the sleaze. "Are you rated on that craft?"

Wade made a simpering grin. "What rating do I need to get the boat out far enough that she'll think twice about swimming back?"

Ice water ran through Kirk's spine and his jaws ground. "Sounds like you have everything planned."

Wade readjusted his shorts. "I don't get many complaints from women her age. I mean, guys like you, what, you're out trolling for hula girls your granddaughter's age?"

Kirk swallowed stinging words.

Wade winked. "When she comes back to work on Tuesday, it'll take a week to wipe the smile off her face."

Kirk walked away from Wade, toward another station and rolled out the exercise ball. "Let me see your Swiss-Ball Jackknife with a push-up."

Wade chuckled, "Better abs, better control."

Kirk stood, arms crossed over his chest, watching Wade eat up the push-ups. "I can see these are familiar routines for you. Let me see what else I've got. No growth in your comfort zone."

Wade flashed his sparkling smile. "Bring it on."

You know, I will.

****

"Are you ready to see House of Double Happiness?" The realtor stood protectively with her back to the Moon Gate doors. "It is especially auspicious for a newly married couple to consider this home. It was built for newlyweds in 1933 and professionally remodeled last year when the original owner's children decided to downsize. Plenty of room for a family, hobbies, fitness..." The realtor's assessing gaze washed over Jax's muscled arms and calves, and then her attention returned to extolling the virtues of a multi-million-dollar home.

****

"Who am I to deny my sweetheart her divine wishes?" Jax chuckled as he opened their resort suite door. Jax strode to the closet and slid hangers of shirts aside, looking for a particular one. "You want to spend that kind of money on a house?" Jax unbuttoned one Aloha shirt and slid on a black, red, and yellow print.

Kameo's animated body language reflected her request. "Double happiness, the name of the house is double happiness. How can we pass that up?"

****

THURSDAY, AUGUST 20TH

Kirk sent the juice barista to the farmer's market for fresh pineapple and began his stint as Smoothie mixologist. Jordan stood, fidgeting with the counter's flyers. Wade's ETA was in three minutes. Just enough time to make some magic. Kirk filled the blender with crushed ice, almond milk, dandelion extract, fresh spinach, chia seeds, apples, blackberries, and avocado. Blended, it looked identical to what Kirk was drinking. Kirk's was minus the colon blow ingredients.

Wade strolled in, no worse for yesterday's wear. He stopped to bump fists with Jordan, and she nodded him over to Kirk at the smoothie bar.

"Since I'm going to put you through the MMA workout today, I thought I'd start you with a power smoothie."

"If we're going intense like that, you think I should drink it now?" He held up the weighty cup.

"Oh, yeah, MMA is incredibly demanding on the body, and you need to be able to generate a tremendous amount of power." Kirk took a long swig of his smoothie, and Wade shrugged and drank his. "You'll need this for the speed and explosiveness in the moves you'll be doing."

****

Wade dragged his Ranger ass to the locker room after forty-five minutes of plyometric push-ups, lunge jumps, and the especially grueling rolling the heavy bag while planking with his knees. After a slow transition off the floor to finish his smoothie, Kirk sent him back for corkscrew planks, seated dumbbell stability punches, and lateral high knees. *If the MMA exercises don't kill him, the trips to the head will slow him down.*

Chapter 5

Watching the security camera on his desktop in his office, Kirk played solitaire on his tablet until he saw Wade enter. The black and white feed made his rival look grey, but that was nothing compared to his 'quart low' pallor when he drag-assed downstairs.

Kirk greeted him with a smoothie of a different color. "This will round you out for your big weekend. Honey, banana, and a touch of cinnamon."

Wade resisted the cup. "What did you give me yesterday?"

Kirk retracted the cup., "Oh, did you want that one again?"

"Like hell. What was in it?"

"Same thing I had, apples, berries, some avocado." Kirk taunted him with this morning's cup, "You're going to like this one."

Wade gave him a slight side-eye as he took it and drew a mouthful. "Okay, nothing like yesterday."

"I like to mix it up, and how do you want to stir up the exercise today?"

Fatigued, Wade shook his head slowly. "It must be the island water. I am an empty vessel today." Kirk heard his feet dragging the mat into the gym.

"Maybe we'll do recumbent bikes, and some floor limbering."

Wade's gut audibly grumbled as he held his abdomen. "Do you think I should exercise feeling like this?"

"Balls to nutsack, you don't look that good, but I'll go easy on you. We'll stay Army level."

****

LAS VEGAS, NEVADA

Desmond Franklin evaded the other barbacks. Since the other night and staff gossip about the explosive applause in the Diamond Room, Des was the butt of some choice jokes. The previously cheap bartenders amped up their greed, reminding Des he made five hundred dollars cash for twenty minutes' work. Mr. DeBlasio's secretary had loose lips, and the word in the casino stretched Des' windfall to thousands by the time he clocked in the next day.

There was a post-it on the employee bulletin board. "Franklin, see Mr. DeBlasio."

"Oooh, who's in trouble now? Use your psychic powers, Des," the secretary taunted as she put her salad in the breakroom fridge. Unperturbed, Des snapped the post-it off the wall and headed into the belly of the beast. He knocked gently.

"Who's there?"

Des pushed the partially open door far enough and stuck in his head. "You wanted to see me, sir?" An Asian man paced near the monitors observing the casino floor below. By his dress and posture, he was the type of man who commanded respect, not anxious fear like Mr. DeBlasio. His boss waved Des in.

"Franklin, have a seat."

Des watched as the tall Asian man sat in the chair beside him. There was an anxious beat of silence, then DeBlasio leaned back in his chair, and laughter roared from his fleshy chest.

"I got to tell you, this kid's 'gift' has to be an act, look at him, shitting in his shoes in the boss's office."

The darkly dressed man gave DeBlasio side-eye and then

nodded to Desmond. "I enjoyed your performance a great deal. When I didn't see you again, I approached Wendall to ask about your performance schedule." There was a beat of anxious silence. "He told me about your contract with the resort." Desmond sat taller as his confidence gathered.

"Mr. Zhao is from Hawaii; he has a fleet of dinner cruises, and he wants to buy out your contract." DeBlasio chortled wickedly.

Des nodded first to DeBlasio and then to Mr. Zhao. "Sir, did Wendall explain my contract to you?"

"That I must buy the remaining time at the rate of fifteen thousand dollars payable to the casino..."

Des sat back in the chair and folded his arms over his chest as he began padding his worth.

"I see, yes, fifteen hundred a week for the remaining ten weeks. But that does not include expenses, the auto lease, the studio apartment, and perdiem meals."

DeBlasio leaned on his elbows and winked at Des. "He's a great headliner, worth every cent." Zhao nodded silently.

"But of course those terms are payable to me. Not the Diamond Room Casino." Des clarified.

DeBlasio narrowed his eyes and winked at Des. He threw up his beefy hands. "The kid didn't get here rolling over. I suggest you take him home with you on your private jet."

Only school keeps me here. There are schools in Hawaii. Who's going to miss my student housing hovel?

Des glanced at Mr. Zhao and knew he was evaluating costs. *The first person to speak loses.* He heard breathing from DeBlasio's obese rattle to his controlled inhalations.

Zhao rose, Des followed suit and watched the man extend his hand. "I leave in two days; can you be ready? Your studio apartment is furnished. We will discuss the performance venue on the flight."

Des felt pure energy in Zhao's handshake. "I'm excited. I've never been to Hawaii."

"We hope you feel the Aloha spirit on our fleet of ships." He handed Des a business card with the flight time and location of the jet at the private airport off the Las Vegas strip.

Chapter 6

Kirk parked his motorcycle in the garage and entered the gym through the utility door. *Silence.* He moped through, flipping on lights, and approving the ship-shape condition of the public areas. He scowled at Jordan's empty spot at the counter. The very thought of her alone with that lech, who might actually get her into bed, kept him up all night.

She's been through my self-defense class. There has to be a dingy on that yacht. She'll be okay. And smarter for it.

As Kirk took slow steps up, he saw the lobby lights flash on. *Mona's here.* The blender whirred, fighting the ice and frozen fruit. *She must be trying Jordan's recipe.*

"Mornin', Mona. Did you make enough for two?" He rounded the stairs.

"It's me. Grab a cup." Jordan dejectedly waited for Kirk before she poured two of her 'wake-up' smoothies.

Kirk cautiously approached the bar and climbed on a barstool. "What are you doing here? You asked for the weekend off."

"Wade IM'd me to say he couldn't get the boat." She poured two cups and frowned.

Kirk watched Jordan's brows knit. "And he couldn't think of something entertaining to do with you on Oahu?"

Jordan propped her chin on her palm. Her spiritless lean on the counter flipped a switch inside Kirk. *What a jackass. He needs to steer clear of this island.*

Jordan stretched and settled in a shrug. "He probably came to the gym to get extra buff for some twenty-something."

"You're better off without him if he's going to play you that way." They stood and sipped. "So, how did you meet him?"

"At a boat show, I won a cooler, and he bought me a drink after the show."

"So, you saw him around his other boating friends? You know, to gauge how he acts around people in public?"

"Not really. He blogs alone. He said these events were where he *circulates*." She made air quotes on the word.

Kirk felt his jaw tighten. "Didn't it strike you odd that you barely knew each other, and he wanted to take you to the middle of the ocean?"

"It was a weekend boat party, where else do you go?" Kirk's heart rate increased, remembering Wade's plans. She studied his face. "Did he say something to you?"

"Let's just say with the vibes I got; I'm glad you took the self-defense class."

Jordan slapped at Kirk's hand. "Why didn't you tell me?"

"What should I have said that he was a bedroom braggadocio? That the entire time he exercised, he correlated it to better sex?"

Jordan sat down hard on the barstool, and her left hand moved across her breasts. "It wasn't supposed to be that kind of party. I mean, I was supposed to share a stateroom with another guest."

"I believe I know who that guest was…"

"Good riddance, then." She marched over to the counter and dragged the anthurium outside the front door and placed it next to the ashtray.

What do you do when you've hurt the person you love to keep her from a deeper hurt?

****

VANCOUVER, CANADA

The woman in the mirror was a stranger. Her hair was too short, with undefined eyebrows and a pale complexion. She felt expressionless. Isabel Huerta 'died' in a fiery boat explosion days ago. In her resurrection as LaDonna Garza-Mendoza, Isabel felt downright dumpy.

When her mansion's ash and cinders settled, Isabel felt she earned every hidden dollar. Her meter began ticking the day the middle-aged widower Guillermo Huerta chose her from her convent school's choir. He was a man who worshipped the concept of marriage. For three years he respected Isabel's virginity and did not marry her until her eighteenth birthday. All the while a candle burned for his deceased first wife.

Cunningly, Isabel found his black book of sexual partners, and her inquisitive sexual tension was spent riding her Azteca stallion, Muerte. By the time she was Guillermo's bride, she wisely chose not to best her husband in chess, but she easily could have, and they both knew it.

Within five years of marriage, he called her his 'worthy counsel' for her sharp intuition while she comported herself as an earnest and docile wife. The gloves came off behind bedroom doors when Isabel gave Guillermo her perspectives on the men within his inner circle. One by one, they were dispensed. Her final disappointment in Guillermo's judgment cost him his life and left her everything. Everything.

By the end of July, with the DEA on her heels, Isabel Huerta moved assets gained from fifty years of Lobos Cartel activity. She was far too young and beautiful to be stressed daily. *Take the money.* Isabel could not have foreseen her disappearance being this easy. Her San Diego lieutenant's tardiness in depositing his weekly take shorted her a paltry thirty-nine million. One thought led to another. *It's the principle of his theft.* He protested her accusal. Inviting the lieutenant, Pollo Phoenix, and his four slack-jawed henchmen to her yacht, luring the self-important idiot into her bed and leaving them all in a fiery explosion was only poetic justice.

Her right hand, known to everyone as Gustavo, mishandled the detonations in her hillside mansion. Gustavo dallied when he should have bolted. He was incinerated. The last loose end was her husband's youngest uncle, Arturo. He was a dear, dear man, but not an 'earner'. When he died in his sleep, Isabel was free.

When Isabel learned Pollo's bank account was hacked, she sent up the flare to her friends in the illegal banking industry. Sensing a reward, they pointed to where the money went, but could not return it. That would be her job. As LaDonna Garza-Mendoza, she was sure her looks and personality would recover once she took back her millions.

****

LaDonna boarded the flight to Honolulu with three well-thumbed Spanish language romance novels in her leather hobo bag.

It was impossible to hide anything of value on a commercial flight. But in plain sight, LaDonna boarded coach class with her eighteen-year-old domestica and an ancient abuela tapping a white cane. Neither of them spoke English and had been instructed to give yes and no answers to any questions in Spanish. LaDonna would do all the talking for her little family.

LaDonna fingered her amethyst rosary all morning. She prayed the Fed Ex package containing her treasure trove of various international passports, bearer bonds, and credit cards in different alternative names would arrive safely at the rental below Fort Ruger Park. She reserved the modest estate on a month to month basis.

Escaping the authorities required a convoluted trip from Mexico to Cuba to Vancouver to Oahu. In truth, Abuela Maria would be handed off to her family upon arrival. Consuela was more an indentured servant than a teen ward. LaDonna promised her convent school this orphan would be treasured and kept pure as her maid and companion. *The nuns are so gullible.*

****

HONOLULU, HAWAII

The house on Papu Circle made LaDonna think of purgatory. Oahu was not Mexico, although people claimed it was paradise. She would get used to the colors primal to the local culture. The home was luxurious and connected to the islands like a tree growing from a rocky crevice. She would adjust to paradise.

Before she 'died', Isabel Huerta did homework and surprised herself. Jax Roman, the stalwart DEA team leader, had secrets. Valuable secrets. Not the least was the location of her thirty-nine million dollars. Jax hid his tracks well, but she knew where his father lived.

****

"Okay, good class today." Kirk Roman clapped large hands at the eight women wilting before him. The fitness expert routinely broke hearts with his chiseled good looks. His steely black and silver hair had a mind of its own. Especially at his sweaty neck. Piercing denim blue eyes mesmerized his class. The women, from the thick-waisted blonde to the trim retiree bathed in sweat, cooled down from fifty minutes of aerobic kickboxing. Kirk tossed his unused towel to the blonde. "Here's a clean towel for you. I didn't use mine."

She caught it with a baleful expression. "No, you never do. What does it take to make you sweat?"

Kirk winked. "Oh, I have my moments." The class grumbled under their breath. "Remember, we are presenting at the Island Fitness show over Labor Day weekend. I hope you all sign up for the demo. We are on center stage Saturday afternoon, and each of you is a fine example of what women can achieve." With exhausted laughter and nodding heads, the group dispersed towards the locker room, and Kirk Roman picked up his clipboard and headed to the front desk. *I love Saturdays, Jordan is here all day.*

"Mr. Roman, you had a phone call, here's the message." Jordan held out a single pink slip between her French manicured fingertips.

Why is she so damn cute? "Just one?"

Jordan nodded her head, her mane of silver hair dusting her shoulders. Her blushing lip gloss reinforced her grin.

"I better renew our advertising…"

"That's at the top of my talking points for Sunday's breakfast."

His chuckle faded as he looked at the name and number. His smile recovered when he looked back at Jordan. "I thought breakfast was supposed to be our time."

"Our time?" She held up a legal pad covered with post-it notes. "So, you want to stay late for these things?"

Kirk kept walking. "Nope, breakfast is on me."

He heard her mutter comically, "It always is…"

****

LaDonna pondered Tolstoy's philosophy as she shopped for athletic wear. The hardest enemy to battle? Impatience. Waiting for planets to align? Science could predict the planets to the instant. Waiting for people to meet? Convergence, when planned artfully, had to be seamless. Otherwise, it set off internal alarms, alerting her mark, Kirk Roman. *Patience.* Mr. Tolstoy said, "The two most powerful warriors are patience and time."

****

"We're working on a couple of options, right now, Dad. Will you be lonely on Mackinac Island, if we decide to stay in Honolulu?"

Dr. Charles Alana, Kameo's father, had been caught twice in the Lobos Cartel's sites. Together the father and daughter were moved to the Lake Huron island months ago. They arrived as uncle and niece, two family practice physicians staffing the island clinic. Despite Isabel's death and the dissolution of the Lobos Cartel, Kameo and her father still kept the cover of assumed names, Doctors Chris, and Casey Adams.

"The Veterinarians outnumber the doctors, but they are very welcoming. I enjoy the slower pace. In a few weeks, the island will be closing for the season. Soon it will be time to learn how to cross-country ski."

Kameo grimaced at the thought of snow. "How's the new physician's assistant working out?"

"He's great, battle-trained. I trust him with my life."

"Battle trained? How rough is that tourist island?"

"He's retired military, and his wife loves horses. We're getting on famously."

"How's Melody? You two still together?"

"Melody recruited Eric out of a sense of selfishness. She wanted me to have a few nights off. He's married to Melody's cousin. We're one big happy family."

"You know, Dad, you and Melody could winter in Oahu if you want to."

"And miss the snowmobiles? Plenty of room for a romantic Christmas if you and Jax come here."

"Daddy, you have this backward, you winter in Hawaii." She stared at the offer on the Double Happiness home. As the savings account interest piled up, she didn't feel guilty about taking her half of the thirty-nine million liberated from the Lobos Cartel. Moving to Hawaii was the right thing. She blended here. Although it was a small island, she could get lost in the throngs of the mixed cultures. *If Jax will calm down and quit behaving as if he's between missions, it will be relaxing.*

****

MONDAY, AUGUST 24

The Lyft driver left Desmond, his two suitcases and three duffle bags in front of an eight-story apartment building. Ornamental concrete blocks in an Asian pattern created dividers between balconies. Plants grew riotously from pots on several floors. He fingered the small envelope with the studio's keys and the parking lot key fob. *Apartment number eight-twelve. I hope there's an elevator, or I won't need this gym on the corner.*

This was no New York Style squashed studio! Yes, the floors were old-style parquet from what century? The futon was in an alcove. If you slept with your head at one end, you woke up with a view of Diamond Head. He had a kitchen full of dishes and even matching glasses. The bathroom wasn't something he wanted to share unless it was with a very good friend, but he was living in Hawaii. For at least ten weeks.

Brochures on the small coffee table in front of the equally small sofa extolled paddleboard and surfing rentals on the other side of Ala Wai Boulevard. Des flexed in the bathroom mirror; he needed better arms for that stuff.

Not a bit jet-lagged, Des unpacked his music collection and speakers, hung his clothes in his closet and tossed a tee-shirt on the futon just to make the place look lived in.

He pulled out the bed and stood in the sleeping alcove. Sliding windows on three sides invited him to sample the island breeze. He opened the windows and took in his panorama. To the left, he saw Diamond Head and the tall, trendy resorts at that end. Below him were working-class apartment buildings and tennis courts. To the right there were more condos and high-rise office buildings and a general buzz of motorcycles and scooters.

Even from a distance, he could feel the rhythm of the breeze as it rolled over the continuous waves. Despite the rows of traffic lights, people were smiling, the pace was dialed down considerably from frantic Vegas, and there was a general sense of relaxation. He'd read it from the folks who arrived in Vegas, called the ninth island because one in ten Hawaiian residents visited Las Vegas every year.

As they parted, Mr. Zhao explained the shaka hand signal for hang loose also meant the number six to the Chinese. "Often, six is used to praise someone who has done well." Therefore, Zhao used the gesture as a parting compliment.

Des enjoyed the idyllic beauty of the island while wondering how to create a sustainable act six days a week. Who did one ask for advice? Maybe, he'd psychically contact Harry Houdini? He had until Thursday night to figure it out. These were the times he wished he could see *his* future. He had no idea what would happen next. But right now, he was going to change into a tee-shirt, shorts, and the flip-flops Hawaiians called slippers for a walk on the beach.

****

Tuesday, September 8th

"You know the time difference is three hours, right, Gid?" Jax growled into the bedside cordless telephone.

"When you understand why the DEA called me back, I think you'll brew yourself a cup of that fancy Hawaiian coffee and listen to my news."

Gideon Sullivan's voice brooked no argument as Jax rolled silently out of bed and pulled the covers back over Kameo. Walking naked through the dark suite, Jax popped a k-cup into the machine. While it brewed, he filled Gideon in on the high points of their trip, their new home, their plans for relocation, and the odd prognostication by the kid in Vegas.

Gideon replied in a series of 'uh-huhs' until Jax chuckled about the seer's words. Once Jax laid a beach towel on the chaise, he stretched out in all his naked glory on the private lanai. "Okay, kill-joy, why did you call at 5:05 AM?"

"Isabel Huerta is alive." There was a stunned silence from Jax. "The fax came after we closed the unit. Sabra loaded the machine around the end of the day, and the fax was in the tray when the new director came in about two hours ago. He called me because you disconnected your cell phone."

"Where is the queen of mean? How do they know? Wasn't she on a BOLO? More seriously, are you back at the DEA task force?"

"She's a ghost. CIA, FBI, INTERPOL, all have nothing on her. The boat had charred remains of five men and one woman. Probably a prostitute, she lured to the boat and poisoned. You know she's a sly dog."

"You didn't answer me; did they rope you into the new task force? Is she your hot item?" Jax heard Gideon grinding his jaw; they had been together long enough for Jax to translate the phone silence.

"Hey, if you hadn't retired, you'd be right back in with me…"

"As bad as I feel about this, Gid, I'd rather be a civilian this time around. I'm out. We're settling in. I am half a world away from Mexico. I haven't heard Spanish since I stepped on this island."

"That's the way you're playing this? That broad has a thirty-nine million-dollar grudge, you and your wife are the last ones standing, and she has all those reasons to take you out."

"Gid, that was less than a quarter of a week's action for her…"

"Since your trip out east and your adventures in married land, a few things have developed." There was a dry silence between the two men, and then Gideon continued. "You knew Uncle Arturo died in his sleep? Our team on the ground says Gustavo was taken out when Huerta's mansion exploded."

"And…"

"And I don't want to get word my friend, and his bride have been snuffed in their sleep." Jax's eyes closed as he remembered the seer's words.

"We're already using different names…"

Chapter 7

"Thank you for the extra help, Mr. Roman." LaDonna thoughtfully touched Kirk's forearm as she turned to leave his gym. "Your pointers gave me insight on executing that move." She nodded self-confidently as she wiped her bright coral towel between her round breasts. Her voice was wicked in smoky tones. She had a habit of looking up at him through long, sooty eyelashes. Her sweat was musky with a cardamom-like incense.

"LaDonna, I could move you into a second class each week if you're up for the challenge." Kirk's attention returned to his clipboard and then swept the gym benches for forgotten items.

"Do you teach that class, too?" The woman posed, wringing her coral towel as Kirk headed toward the door. He looked over his shoulder, giving a non-verbal prompt that class was over, and lights were going out in three, two, one second. The woman nearly skipped to catch up to him.

"No, Avery teaches that class…"

"Is he as skilled as you?" She purred.

Kirk made longer strides from his hanger-on and answered over his shoulder about to duck into his office. "Avery is retired military; she's actually better tuned to how you would execute the moves. Check with Jordan at the desk, okay?"

****

Jordan felt the air change from island calm to traffic jam turbulence. *Here comes the maneater. Who drew this redhead so badly and what did I do to deserve her coming my way?*

Jordan stood; fingers perched on the keyboard. LaDonna came to a stop in front of the counter and spread her hands out, claiming as much space as possible. "Kirk says I should consult you about taking more classes."

Jordan basked in the knowledge of her power, and a sweet smile erupted on her lips. "Well, what results do you seek?"

LaDonna looked confused. The redhead drilled a long index fingernail into her wild hairdo and posed. "Well, I want to improve my stamina and my core strength. What other classes does Mr. Roman teach?"

Jordan returned to studying the class list on her monitor. She flipped through spreadsheets of classes and their students. "Kirk," and Jordan paid extra emphasis on using his first name, "teaches the Warrior class on Tuesdays and Thursdays, but of course you have to take the prerequisites for that class."

LaDonna stood back and stroked at her breastbone, nostrils flared. "You make it sound like a university."

Jordan tilted her head like Gidget. "Are you at least a brown belt?"

"Well, no…"

"You wouldn't qualify. Then, would you consider Crash *LIVE?*"

LaDonna squinted at Jordan. "Crash? *LIVE?*"

Jordan drummed her sensibly manicured nails on the counter and droned on with the class description. "Crash *LIVE* is the cardio-based, athletic-style workout that combines the best of high-intensity interval training and strength moves intended to get you fit fast." Jordan looked over her readers at LaDonna, preening in the mirror behind the counter. "There is an age limit, are you under fifty?"

LaDonna bristled and announced coldly, "Considerably under fifty."

Jordan made math calculating motions with her finger as she looked carefully at the class requirements. "Because this class gives you total-body benefits, every sweaty class improves your strength, endurance, and agility. But you have to be measured prior to being accepted for the class."

"Measured?" LaDonna shrilled.

Jordon nodded thoughtfully. "According to the World Health Organization, the waist to hip ratio for healthy women is 0.85 or less. However, for this class, Kirk insists women must be 0.80 or less."

LaDonna threw up her hands. "What does that even mean?"

Jordan pointed to the current class on the tv monitor. "See the girl in pink? She's a good example."

"What is she, fourteen?"

"She's actually nineteen… Isn't she the cutest little button?" Jordan pitched a no-hitter. Every one of Kirk's classes were so high achieving or extremely focused that LaDonna couldn't pick up another with him. "If you enjoyed having Kirk as an instructor, you should count your blessings. He's covering that class until Barbra comes back from maternity leave."

Jordan watched the dragon lady wilt with each sentence. *Score one for the old grey-haired lady.* LaDonna left, a pale shell of herself.

****

Kirk locked his office door. *How do famous personalities handle this?* Kirk realized his looks and charm were highly linked to the success of the gym. There were more men than women on Oahu, *but where the hell are they?* Eighty percent of his classes were women, no matter how many demographics directed advertising campaigns he held. LaDonna was the angsty over-achiever of the season. If he met her at a Waikiki bar, he didn't think she'd give him the time of day, but here, he couldn't shake her.

Kirk dimmed the office lights and closed his private bathroom door. He dialed his tensions back with more relaxing music. Elvis, in his late fifties sound with the driving guitars and angst-ridden voice. As Kirk stood under the pulsing shower, he slipped into a fantasy hearing the King croon, "One night with you is what I'm now praying for." That was the theme song for teenage lust in the era of Wally and the Beaver.

If only I lived in the fifties and Jordan was the girl next door. He closed his eyes and saw himself picking her up for prom. He felt his knees knock as he imagined stepping up to the front door, corsage box in hand. He looked top drawer in his white dinner jacket. His best dress shoes were mirror bright.

Jordan's pipe-smoking father answered the door. The man's expression was not welcoming as the pipe bobbed with his greeting, "Come in, son." He led Kirk to the library, where a large black lab slept next to a wing chair.

Kirk stood awkwardly while Jordan's insurance executive father lectured him. "Young man, you stand on the threshold of adulthood. Tonight you will get a taste of adult responsibility. You know why?" The man didn't give Kirk a chance to answer. "Because I expect you to treat Jordan like the lady she is. Her curfew is one in the morning. No lollygagging, have you got that?"

Watching the man's pipe bob with each word, Kirk swallowed hard. "Yes, sir." When he caught the scent of Evening in Paris, he turned to the archway. There she stood. His angel. Even if it was just for one night, they were a couple. He felt her parent's scrutiny as he slid the dyed carnation corsage on her left wrist. She daintily inhaled the scent. "Oh, Kirk, my favorite. Pink carnations."

"Your mom told my mom you were wearing a pink dress. I hoped it would be the right shade."

With admonitions to have a nice time and be 'good', the door to the home closed behind them, and he guided her walk to his dad's freshly waxed car. With God only knew how many yards of pink tulle gathered in Jordan's lap, he closed the door and began breathing again.

"Gee, Jordan, you look swell. Did your hair take a long time?"

Jordan pushed a bobby pin tighter into her ornate updo and smiled demurely. "It was all worth it if you like it, Kirk."

They drove a while in silence, and then Kirk cleared his throat to speak. "I leave for basic training the week after graduation. I sure would like a memory to take with me."

Innocently she bubbled, "This certainly will be a night for me to remember. You're so handsome, Kirk."

He cautiously approached a yellow traffic light and stole a kiss on her cheek at the intersection. When the car started again, she pulled her compact from her evening bag. "If I'd have seen that coming, you would have ruined my lipstick."

"I never want to ruin you in any way." Kirk heard himself utter the words and blushed furiously.

"Oh, Kirk…" she purred.

****

As Kirk dried off, he shook off the fifties' fantasy. He never experienced that innocence. He was a teen in the late seventies. His dad was an enlisted man. Kirk was the bonus baby after his parents sent three other kids to high school. Dad was at sea, so an older mom ruled life on base. If Kirk wanted a new life, he'd have to make it himself.

He wouldn't score a good woman like Jordan in a lottery. What would she want with an ex-con? A veteran of a bad marriage and a broken family?

It was Saturday around four, and he was taking his snorkeling gear up to Kuilima Cove. He needed the mental clarity the water would infuse. He was comfortable there; the water was cool and blue. It would be him, the fish, and the tourists. He changed into jams and a gym tee-shirt. *I have to represent my brand* and happily whistled as he left for the parking garage.

****

There she was, leaning against a black late-model BMW with a flat tire, her cellphone to her ear. LaDonna's titian hair was gelled and spiky, and she'd added rose gold plumeria earrings. The matching necklace bobbled in the crease of her cleavage. Out of that sports bra and into more alluring underwear, there was considerable cleavage.

Kirk noticed her bright coral toes peeping out from low rose gold Springolator pumps. She was Sandy from Grease dropped into tight Hawaiian print capris and halter top, and there was no Danny to come to her aid. *Or is that my role?* She was involved in a hushed but animated conversation.

Kirk opened the saddlebag on his Road King, quietly dropped his gear in and pulled on his helmet. He threw a long leg over his Wicked Red and Twisted Cherry Harley and prepared to duck out. As he fired up all 1746 CCs with a throaty roar, LaDonna waved frantically, her frown enhanced by her knitted brow and pursed lips.

Kirk pulled within a few feet and got a better look at the flat tire and the lady in distress. "Someone on their way?" *Give me peace, give me solitude, please have a motor club coming.*

"I didn't transfer my auto club when I moved. It's going to be later tonight before they can get out. Would you believe a two-hour backlog?" Her dramatic gestures tapped at his internal knight. "It would be safe here overnight, wouldn't it?"

Kirk shook his helmeted head and spoke over the bike's engine. "Not really. They tow vehicles after nine; the apartments upstairs need the space. You have a jack and a spare?"

****

Kirk wiped his hands on the terry towel that wrapped around the jack in LaDonna's trunk. Nothing like changing tires with a full-size spare after a day of leading six hours of kickboxing and body-sculpting.

"Let me buy you dinner?" LaDonna shrugged her tanned shoulders. "With a body like yours, you do eat, don't you?"

Kirk smothered a chuckle. He was hungry as hell, and he'd forgotten about that when he initially set out to go snorkeling. He checked his watch. "It is about that time. Any place special in mind?"

"I've been here for two weeks. What do you suggest?" She posed close to his bike.

Kirk stroked his five o'clock shadow and thought. "Have you eaten at Side Street yet?" The woman's shoulders rose and fell as she shook her head. Kirk donned his helmet and flipped up the mask. "Follow me." He started his bike and missed her disappointment at not being asked to hang onto him on the Road King.

****

Somewhere between his Ahi Poké, her Lilikoi Baby Back Ribs, and a few cocktails, LaDonna began the habit of reaching across the booth's table to touch Kirk's hand.

"Try this," Kirk encouraged as he held up a fork of the zesty sushi-grade ahi tuna. LaDonna caught his hand in both of hers and guided it into her mouth. She aimed her admiring gaze right at Kirk with his genial enthusiasm for great Poké.

She made sensuous noises, still holding his hand and the empty fork. "Like it?" He asked needlessly, extracting his hand, and pushing his bowl closer to her.

If flirting was governed by a complex set of unwritten laws of etiquette, this woman had not read the book. Without discussion, LaDonna swiftly slid from her side of the booth to his, playfully hip bumping him as she landed. "I appreciate a man who watches out for women… who can change a tire and feed her hungry… body."

Kirk's head snapped to her at his side. After an appraising gaze, his smile traveled all the way up to his eyes. "I'll bet you do." Was it something he'd done to invite her attention? Had he grown so worried about causing offense or sending the wrong signals at the fitness center he lost his natural talent for playful, harmless flirtation? Or, did this new woman come to town set on saving the human race from extinction, by preserving Kirk Roman's lineage?

****

LaDonna led him on a furious ride to her Papu Circle home. The formidable woman braced herself in the front doorway. "Is this what I think it is?" Her voice was husky, born of time-tested hunger.

Kirk's arms rose to catch her hands to pin her in that doorway. "What do you think this is?"

She bowed her back to press closer to Kirk. "Dessert?"

"Dessert, a midnight snack and hopefully breakfast in bed."

CHAPTER 8

Kirk slipped out of LaDonna's bed before sunrise. *Man, that woman can test a fella.* She may not have arranged for her motor club membership, but she arrived with quite a few bedroom toys. Kirk wondered if the entire armoire was full of them.

He hadn't ditched her; he left a note thoughtfully penned on island print notepaper he found hanging on the inside of a kitchen cabinet. Leaving it on the pillow, he left silently. He walked his bike to the end of the long driveway and then roared off.

She wore him out. Although he was probably one of the fittest fifty-nine-year-old men in the state, he'd had to tap his stash of little blue pills around midnight. Good thing the lady had a selection of condoms that rivaled a druggist.

On the ride back to his peaceful perfection by the sea, Kirk dickered with himself over LaDonna. It could have been a physical facepalm if he hadn't required both hands on his bike handles. No way he could keep her on the down-low at the gym. He had visions of rabbits in stewpots if he tried to cool down this woman. *Then why did I go back for seconds and thirds? I don't even want to count the condom wrappers.*

She was a machine, built for comfort all the way. What was she, maybe late thirties, early forties? Every limb was lithely muscled, hinting at her being a horsewoman or a fencer. She said it had been a long time. She didn't seem out of practice. Hell, when was the last time he met a woman this ripe?

As the sun crept over Diamond Head, Kirk parked his bike inside the garage and took the steps to the oceanside mansion.

Keying the security code into the door, he watched a lizard scamper into the lush foliage.

It was Sunday; he'd shower, shave, and meet Jordan for their customary breakfast at The Highway Inn. Perhaps later this morning, he'd call the number on the pink slip. If Casey Rawlings was right about his son being on the island, he should gather the gumption to connect with Jax. He'd carried that weight too long.

****

Jordan dropped Stevia into her tea as Kirk slunk into the restaurant. His pumped physique hinted at an early morning workout, but the haunted expression in his eyes was at odds with his loose-jointed grace. He was showered and shaved and fragrant to the point that she expected a film crew for a commercial.

Kirk slid into the booth with lips curiously curled downward. If this were a fragrance ad, would it be Mortification? *How would that smell?*

"Good morning, handsome. Did you do all this for me?" She waved her index finger over him like a wand.

"All what?" His inner grump emerged.

"You look different for a Sunday morning. Usually, you're all loose and casual…"

He cut her off, palm flat on the table. "I'm loose. I'm casual."

"Uh-huh. Okay. So, what's for breakfast?"

The server brought Kirk's usual black coffee, and he waved away the menu. "Four egg omelet, whole wheat toast, a slice of ham, and yah got strawberries?" The server nodded and disappeared.

"Hungry boy today? How long did you snorkel yesterday? Did you ever come up for air?"

Kirk's cobalt gaze narrowed. "What do you mean by that?"

"You were going to snorkel yesterday, that didn't go well?"

"What's on the agenda?" He growled.

****

"Let me send you the address…" Kirk closed the brief phone call with Casey. His mouth ran dry at the sight of her as they face-timed. His son's wife? *Of course, he'd find a brilliant and beautiful woman.* He caught her visible surprise when he answered the call poolside. Kirk not only had to process that his son was moving to the island, but that he'd recently resigned his commission and married. *Too many years gone. Was there a relationship to salvage?*

****

"Sweet Jesus, Mary, and Joseph." Jax whistled as he turned off Diamond Head Road into what could only be a mansion built on a sliver of earth over the ocean. "How the fuck did he fall into this?" Jax's head snapped around as he parked.

Kameo sat gobsmacked by the opulence of the three-story home that hugged the incline to the water. Jax parked their rental convertible under the stately porte-cochre, and together they stared down the series of broad steps to a pair of arched frosted glass doors confidently thrown wide open. Kameo placed a calming hand on Jax's. "Listen to whatever he has to say."

"Yeah, just count to ten before I follow my urge to wipe the deck with him. Remind me again why you thought this was a good idea?" Jax's gaze narrowed past Kameo as he saw the silhouette he remembered as his father.

"Harboring hatred toward Kirk does more than keep him in the doghouse. You get stuck there, too, forever the child, the victim, the have-not in a world of love."

"Okay, Doctor. Drop the therapy talk, and let's see what he has to say."

"As your wife and your partner, I ask you whether you choose to live in the past or the present? Think about what a present this is becoming." Kameo kissed two fingers and pressed them to Jax's straight lips.

She caught Jax's hand as they descended the steps. She watched the two men weigh each other in their identical pensive stares. *This is going to be an adventure.* Jax stood about an inch taller than Kirk, their builds similarly impressive from years of conditioning. Kirk's silver hair shown against his deep tan. The two men shared the same smile lines at the eyes, poetic lips, and cleft chins.

"Dad," Jax's voice was dry, "This is my wife, Casey." His posture straightened, and he turned to her. "Baby, this is Kirk Jackson Roman."

****

Kameo's jaw dropped as Kirk led them across smooth wood floors through bright ivory, view-filled rooms. The walls, devoid of art or personal images, were the frames for the panorama of swaying palms, azure skies, low stone walls, and the endless ocean. One interior wall sported Brazilian ebony shelving holding state of the art audio components.

As they followed him through the home on highly polished ebony floors, Kirk reflexively picked up the remote and turned on Elvis. Without seeing the speakers, it sounded as if they were present at the Aloha from Hawaii concert.

"Inside or out?" Kirk asked as he poured sparkling water into tall glasses at the bar of the lanai kitchen.

Jax pointed to the large tiles of the covered lanai. "Is this considered in or out?" Kameo caught a hint of dry sarcasm and tucked her chin.

Kirk chuckled. "If you're from the mainland, it's hard to get used to all these open rooms. Let's head over to the pool." He hoisted a tray on one hand and led them past a cascading water feature with ornate mosaics. In the garden's simplicity, it was luxuriously primal.

Jax sat erect on the teak lounge chair as Kameo sniffed along the hedge. "This beats back home, doesn't it?"

Kirk rubbed his thumb along his jaw as his appraising gaze swept his son. "In a heartbeat. Do I understand you're relocating here?" Kirk leaned back on the low volcanic rock wall. His tanned forearms were folded high on his chest.

Jax dropped his face low over his glass and scanned for Kameo. When she didn't answer, Jax spoke. "In the process of buying a home not too far from here. But it all comes with a secret. You can't talk about us." Kameo registered Kirk's wide-eyed nod. "In fact, we're using the names, Jason and Casey Rawlings."

"Does it have something to do with your resigning your commission?" Kirk watched the two become more guarded, and they moved to be together.

"Yeah, but you don't know anyone who knows Jax Roman. If you talk about us, just separate Jason and Casey from the family."

Kirk closed his eyes and drew in a couple of deep breaths.

"Now that Jax is retired and I came into a little money, we bought a home. We thought it was something we should grab before housing starts another rise." With a sweeping glance at the home and the water view, she smiled. "Have you been here long? This home is utterly glamourous."

Kirk's gaze shifted right to the ocean and then back to a turquoise door on a small building between the home and the hedges. "Here? Yeah, about sixteen years." He scratched at his neck and smiled. "You kids hungry?"

****

"You kids hungry?" Jax parroted as he held the suite door open for Kameo. "Nobody's cooked in that kitchen in ten years." He stomped over to the bar and twisted the top off a beer, held it up to Kameo, and when she shook her head, he drank down half of it. "I'm going to be up all night trying to figure out how a guy comes out of prison, moves to Oahu, and makes out as he has." Jax picked up the tourist magazine on the end table and sailed it across the room. "Is my father mobbed up?"

"It was gracious of you to pay for supper." Kameo smiled.

"And then talking until five forty-five when he conveniently had reservations for three at Chef Hilo at six PM? You're telling me…"

"What did we agree, babe?" Kameo opened sparkling water and tilted her head sharply before she drew on the bottle.

"…to hold on to the knowledge of his love for me, and my love for him." Jax went to gesture with the beer bottle, and he collapsed on the brightly colored ottoman. He made a fist and laughed. "I can't wait until you unload all the body language you deciphered, please tell me your shrink sense was tingling."

Kameo stood on the threshold between the living room and the shady lanai. "News at eleven, okay?"

****

TUESDAY, SEPTEMBER 15TH

"I don't know how to repay you for convincing Jax to come over Sunday." Kirk's enthusiasm for Kameo's call was evident in his tone.

"Keep up with the baby steps, Kirk. You have to understand…"

"That Jax is skittish."

She reinforced the name change. "Jason, Jason is skittish. That's a nice way of saying that, Kirk. I want you to know; I am dropping the go-between role, from here out, I need you to call

66

him. Meet him at the beach; he still has that annoying wake-up and run habit."

"Beach? Sunrise? I can do that. Just don't be a stranger, Casey."

****

Jordan absentmindedly folded towels. The television monitors in the gym were tuned to the closed cable channel with Kirk Roman's Ten Steps to Fitness. Jordan knew how long-ago Kirk filmed the video because she was the woman in the back row, newly widowed, wearing all black, trying to look less than two hundred and twenty-five pounds. It took Jordan three days a week for two years to get in the best shape of her life.

She no longer weighed herself. She ate what she liked in sensible portions and enjoyed living outdoors. What was round was firm, and what was lithe was tanned. She gave up hair dye and makeup for sunscreen and traded her SUV for a convertible with a bike rack.

Everything was peaceful at nine this morning. The sunrise aerobics had come and gone. Jordan enjoyed the time between the rabid aerobicizers and the moms who left their toddlers next door to join in body sculpting.

These days Jordan was in control. She slept well, and once she expedited her husband's estate, she lived well in a two-bedroom high rise on Kapiolani avenue.

Did she want a man? The one man she wanted was the adored Kirk Roman. He was attentive without being a sleaze. He was fatherly, brotherly, and kindly without being wimpy. Today, she came into her job at Silver SEAL Fitness with a particular hunger for a date with the boss. Was it something about the way he stole second glances at her over his shoulder? When did she begin noticing him that way?

It had to have something to do with LaDonna Garza-Mendoza. That witch blew into the gym five minutes ago, fairly glowing. Entirely made up, she barely made eye contact with Jordan as she waved her key tag under the scanner. *Yeah, girl, I see the nasty original photo we snapped when you signed up. Today you're made up like RuPaul's Drag Race.*

Kirk jogged up the outside stairs and smiled his nine to five smile. "Good morning, Jordan, was I an ass Sunday morning?"

That was not the same question he posed every Tuesday morning. Jordan took Mondays off. She shook her head, "No, there was just something off; we never talked about it." She gestured down the stairs. "Heat-seeking missile loaded and waiting down there."

Kirk's lips moved silently, "La-Don-na?"

Jordan chuckled. "Uh-huh. So far, we have six for this morning's class, two no-shows." She looked at the clock. "Better get your motor running, boss."

Jordan couldn't remember Kirk ever sleeping with a client. For months after joining the fitness center, she'd hung on for dear life to have their Sunday breakfast meetings at the Highway Inn. *He never touched me.* Even as the pounds melted off. *I'm an idiot. That redheaded trollop marched right in here with the air she owned the joint. And she does. Great.*

****

After days of a strong internal dialog about the need for fitness and the fact that every other guy on the island looked like a swimsuit model, Des headed for the fitness club eight floors below him.

What a lazy ass, I'm taking the elevator down. At least the windows are dark, and they don't exhibit our shortcomings to the public. Des entered the gym mesmerized by all the apparatus spaced along the walls. Mirrors created an army of gym rats where there were only two. *Oh, dear, God, I look like I can barely open mayonnaise jars next to them.*

"May we help you?" Two women smiled at Des like he was a cupcake on a dessert buffet. One was probably his age, but the other was his mother's age, and she wore a more wolfish smile.

Des carried the flyer from his apartment and handed it to the mother wolf. The younger girl twirled a lock of hair and sighed as he drew closer. "I'm Bobbie; you live in this building?"

Des was struck dumb. The mother wolf picked up the flyer. "Yes, this is a resident pass. Basic membership is included in your rent. If you wish to take accelerated classes, you get a fifty percent discount, too. What brings you into Silver SEAL Fitness today?"

"Ah, I want to, ah… do that thing on the surfboard with the paddle." There was a beat of silence among the three of them.

"Excuse my manners; my name is Jordan." She extended her hand to Des. *Wow, she is the penultimate gym mom.* All of his inhibitions about being there dissolved. "Bobbie can walk you through the machines after we get your information in the system. Do you have workout gear?"

Des felt her scrutiny from the worn-out Las Vegas resort tee-shirt to the cut off denim shorts down to his slippers. "I just moved here, and no, I don't."

Jordan nodded at him and pointed. "You could get away with the tee-shirt, but those shorts would constrict you, and flip flops aren't safe in a gym."

Bobbie nearly bounced over the counter. "We've got some great workout gear at the boutique right behind you. And there's a shoe store around the corner." She leaned in conspiratorially. "Their sneakers are half what ours are."

Des felt unexpectantly welcome. Bobbie had obviously taken advantage of the gym's employee benefit to work out. She was as built as the showgirls in Vegas, and it looked all-natural to him. She was a fox with gleaming dark hair and a blinding smile. He smiled back. "Are you one of the trainers?"

"If you want yoga and body sculpting, I am." She came from behind the counter and led Des to the boutique where an eerily familiar cutout stood against a wall. The seriously fit cardboard man held up a canister of some supplement.

"Where have I seen this guy?" Des pointed to the cutout. "Who's that?"

Bobbie laughed. "That's the boss, Kirk Roman."

"Is it going to take me until I'm his age to get that fit?"

Bobbie grinned. "He came out of the service like that and just kept it up."

"I want to be fit, but I don't want to look like a spectacle in a sideshow."

Bobbie ran a hand down his upper arms. "Lean muscle is what you want. We can help you with that." Her brown eyes twinkled at him as he caught her hand to hold it. When he placed his other hand over hers, he saw snatches of her life.

"You're a college student, so am I. What are you studying?"

She never tried to pull her hand away. "Physical therapy."

"Do you like living in the dorm?" She eased her hand away and gave him a dubious look. "I haven't registered for school over here yet. I'm on a ten-week contract as a mentalist."

That word caused her to tilt her head in curiosity. "No way! Is that how you picked up stuff about me? 'Cause for a minute, I thought you were a nut."

Des laughed. "That's debatable. But, yeah, I could see you going to school and the dorm. If this gig lasts longer than ten weeks, I might register and finish here."

Bobbie covered her gaping mouth. "So, you're like a psychic, a performer, like in a show?"

He blushed at her effusive comment. "Yeah, it's a dinner cruise, it's not like I'm the Amazing Kreskin, but I am Xavier the Oracle." Des reached into his back pocket for his wallet and produced a ticket. "This ticket is good for two for a weekday dinner cruise. I'd love to hear your feedback."

Bobbie took the ticket and tapped it on her palm. She leaned closer. "Can you tell me if the guy I'm seeing is on the level?"

Des blushed. "I'd rather not."

"Why not?"

He shifted from foot to foot. "Because my answer might be affected by my feelings."

"Are you flirting with me, Mr. Oracle?"

"Are you serious about the other guy?"

Her two hands balanced like a scale. "Ehh."

"Would you like to meet across the street for coffee someday?" He nodded to the coffee shop across the intersection.

****

"I like an independent man." LaDonna purred at the end of class as the other students left for the locker room.

Kirk looked over his shoulder as he flipped switches on the microphone system his aerobics instructor would use for the lunch class. "Glad my note didn't upset you."

LaDonna posed seductively out of arm's length so Kirk could see her full figure encased in spandex. "I enjoyed dinner … and dessert." Her tongue swept her top lip.

71

"It certainly was out of the ordinary for me. You are a firecracker." Kirk took precautions to hold things in his arms, a class book, a towel, anything to keep LaDonna from reigniting the sparks that flew between them.

"A man like you, well, he has to be in high demand. I was wondering if I could invite you to dinner some night this week…"

"I'm glad you understand my position. This isn't a great week."

She purred. "Thursday, your last class ends at five. Perhaps then?"

"Can I get back to you on Wednesday if that's not too short a notice?"

With a quick raise of her brow and a shrug, LaDonna acquiesced.

CHAPTER 9

"Good thing, the house was vacant." Jax huffed as he drove his vintage, stripped-down camo Jeep onto his paver driveway.

Kameo looked at the surrounding estates. *How is a young couple with a Jeep going to be received in a neighborhood of multi-million-dollar homes?* "Yeah." She wrapped her arms around her backpack with the real estate papers.

"Feels funny renting our house from the owners until the closing." Jax jumped out and dug for the door code. As they approached the wrought iron Moon Gate, Jax surprisingly hoisted Kameo in his arms and carried her to the front door.

"You didn't have to carry me this far." She protested as Jax keyed the four-digit entry code into the doorknob plate.

"Yeah, I did." Jax toed open the door and dramatically stopped. Both of them were struck silent by the vast, empty rooms of warm, dark wood on the floors and ceilings.

"Can you believe this is ours?" Kameo whispered.

Jax chuckled. "I thought there would be more. Where's the furniture?" He put her feet on the floor and nuzzled her neck.

Kameo blanched. "Oh, they sent back the staging furniture."

"Hell, call 'em up, get it back."

"It would be easier to go back to the resort and get a room."

Jax turned a circle, hands on hips, in his cavernous living room. "We paid how many millions, and its unfurnished? I thought it was all-inclusive."

Kameo bit her lip. "It was turnkey, but I confess, I thought they'd leave us a standing lamp."

Jax wandered the empty house, his voice echoing back to Kameo. "What do we do now?"

****

MONDAY, OCTOBER 12TH

Kameo drove Jax nuts attending furniture auctions. When he finally gritted his teeth, one day, she dropped him off at Lēʻahi Beach Park, around the corner, and sped off in her new truck.

Hours later, she returned and headed poolside to find Jax swimming laps in their pool while an American Pit Bull mix chased him on the patio. "Doobie," Jax called, and the dog stood at attention. "This is the missus. Whatever she says goes, get it?" The brown and white dog cocked his head, floppy ears still moving and yawned. Jax launched out of the pool and bent to the dog. "Got it?" He clipped a leash on Doobie's red collar and walked him to Kameo. The dog sat, waiting for her attention. Jax winked and nodded to the dog. "He's a good boy."

"Where did you get this good boy?" Kameo hedged around the sniffing pup.

"Hey, they gave me two Loco Moco, not a pork plate and a…" The stranger in jams coming from the house was a guy with a surfer's body. He carried a tray with two dinners like a carhop. Kameo followed her nose and circled the plates and the stranger.

"You went to the Rainbow Drive-In without me?"

"She's a keeper, no comment about the dog, she's more upset about a plate of food." Gideon sat the tray down on the table and scratched at two day's blonde stubble.

Jax toweled off and caught Kameo for a kiss on her neck. "Baby, this is Gideon Sullivan."

****

Gideon Sullivan followed Kameo into the kitchen. "I'm sorry about the food. When I called, he said he didn't know how long you'd be out."

Kameo leaned back against the counter and folded her arms over her tank top. "I'm good, seriously. By the way, thanks for getting me that message when I called the DEA in a tizzy."

Gideon looked over his shoulder, outside, and then back to her. "Tizzy? Yeah, your husband can put the sanest people into a tizzy." He gestured as he spoke, his hands punctuating his words. "Glad you could read between the lines. After working with your husband for three years on the DEA taskforce I had a few of those tizzies myself."

Kameo spoke softly. "You were the team member from the Marshals Service, right?"

Gideon kept looking back at Jax and the dog. "Right. I was the fugitive hunter." He was half in this conversation and half observing Jax.

"Does your being here mean *she's* here?" Kameo turned away and dug in the refrigerator for leftovers.

Gideon's silence went so far, and then he called Jax from the pool. "Hey, boss. We need you in the kitchen."

Doobie padded into the house and shook, looked around for approval, and then curled up by a plasticware bowl of water. "Oh, look, Doobie thinks he's the boss." Kameo popped food in the microwave and watched Jax towel off.

"Yeah." Gideon folded his arms over his chest, shoulders hunched, hands into his armpits.

Jax entered the kitchen. "The body language doesn't look so good. Are we talking about Huerta?"

"The lady did ask."

"Then, the lady needs to know." Jax pulled out a chair and motioned to them. The microwave beeped, and Kameo brought her leftovers to the table.

Gideon's gaze passed back and forth between Jax and Kameo as she raised her fork. "Am I about to lose my appetite?"

Gideon folded his hands on the table and drew in a deep breath. "Hope not... Isabel Huerta did not die in the boat explosion. Subsequent analysis showed it was a prostitute planted on the boat with Phoenix and his four flunkies..."

Jax tipped back in the chair. "The same four we had in custody?"

"Yup. Anyway, international banking investigations showed she made transfers to other offshore accounts for days before she blew up her yacht. Her assets from settling the leveled home and the yacht were distributed to a convent school in Mexico." Kameo ate and shook her head while she chewed. "Her ship crew was 'placed' with a Saudi Sheik." There was a moment of silence between the three. "The captain now owns a fleet of fishing boats in the Maldives."

"And she's long gone with no leads?" Kameo put down her fork, propped her elbows on the table and covered her face."

"Gid, we're here as Jason and Casey Rawlings..."

Gideon put up a hand. "Yeah, and that's all good. Jonah and Norah have done a great job. The SNAFU is Isabel probably relocated before we put out the facial recognition request. Hell, she could have had extensive cosmetic surgery with her money. Alice Walton is worth forty-four billion, but that's legal income. We have no way of knowing Isabel's true assets. That thirty-nine million Norah clipped for you was a quarter of a week's income."

"We installed state-of-the-art security here..." Jax pointed to the censors at every egress.

"Yeah, but you moved to an island, a small island, and everything is wide open here." Gideon waved a hand at the open floor plan, large windows, and mountainside location as he shook his head.

"But, my wife blends in, if I'm wearing a cap, I blend in." Jax retorted.

Kameo rested her chin on her palm as she darted her gaze between the men. "How long are you here? Are you setting up a team? Is this San Diego all over again?"

"The local authorities are aware of Huerta's disappearance. I have not alluded to your living here." Gideon bit his bottom lip. "No one can know your true identities. If there's a traitor as there was in San Diego, we might as well buy a blimp to anchor over your roof."

"So, what are the new rules?" Kameo bit her pinkie nail.

Gideon chuckled and looked to Jax. "Oh, you haven't explained those? How long have you been married, and she doesn't know Roman's Rules?"

Jax rose from his chair and hid for a moment behind the fridge door. "I'm not like that anymore; I'm retired..."

"Oh, hell, yeah, you're retired. Then why is your hair still high and tight? Jeesh, If I were out here, I'd have a beard and a ponytail by now." Gideon watched silent communication pass between the newlyweds, and he stifled a laugh. "I'm gonna check-in at the hotel near the university and visit with Flint and Mavis…Maybe have some dinner."

Jax was on Gideon in a heartbeat. "Flint Tomas opted out to become a university instructor. Do not drag him back into this!" Jax held up his index finger, the old warning gesture.

Gideon caught it with both hands and moved it out of his face. "What rule is this? I'm a little hazy 'cause you're retired now…"

****

Kameo leaned back against her soaking tub's padded neck pillow. It was becoming increasingly difficult to relax in her garden tub with Jax's self-appraising 'hmms' and 'nahs'. Jax stood drip drying in front of his bath vanity.

His ass is mighty fine. She wished she could convince him to sunbathe in the buff. *We have an eight-foot fence!* But he insisted on knee-length jams. *They could see his white ass from the top of Diamond Head.* "What are you doing?" The hmms and nahs continued. "Jax, what are you doing?"

He looked back at her in the mirror. "Huh?" His fingers pressed back along the sides of his head as he turned this way and back to test a new haircut.

"You're talking to yourself, what's going on?"

He dropped his hands to his side and blushed. "Oh, Gideon took me to a stylist when he got a haircut. The girls at the shop all said I'd look great in this undercut thing." He put his hands back up to demonstrate skin instead of hair. "They shave it on the sides and let the top grow…"

Kameo launched from the tub trailing bubbles. "Don't you dare. I swear, Jax Roman, we'll be in divorce court if you ever mutilate yourself that way."

Jax looked bewildered. "What? They all said…"

"No!" Her hands cupped his military haircut. "Grow it out. I want something to run my fingers through, something to hold onto beside your ears." She wiggled her brows at him as she dripped bathwater on his feet.

Jax grabbed her ass with both hands and drew her up, nose to nose. "Oh, yeah, you think I'd be sexy with longer hair?" He arched a brow and posed in the vanity mirror like James Bond with his woman.

"Oh, yeah, baby. You'd rock longer hair." She nestled her cheek on his chest and played with his nipple. Parts of him woke up.

"Rad, I can feel my follicles growing." His grin was adorably cheesy.

"I don't think that's your follicles."

"Indulge me, show me what you'd do if I had longer hair."

****

They cuddled in the king-size bed on their tummies, watching the fish in their saltwater aquarium. Jax drew lazy circles on her back. "That damn thing was too much to move. They left Nemo behind. What's on your agenda for tomorrow? More furniture auctions?"

Kameo wrinkled her nose and made a noncommittal sound. "Actually, I have an interview at a family free clinic tomorrow. They're looking for a part-time doctor."

Jax's head jerked from the peaceful view, and his lips curled downward. "Oh?"

"I can't buy furniture for the rest of my life. Sooner or later, you'd expect me to get something done."

"But work? I thought we were the idle rich." He rolled on his side and propped his head on his hand.

"Jax, I'm only thirty years old. I've spent most of my life in school studying to be what I want to be. I like being a doctor." Jax looked glum. "There must be something you want to do. You'll wear out the pool furniture."

Jax flopped on his back as if the ceiling had the answer. "I've spent my life learning tactical maneuvers and intelligence. What am I supposed to do, start a neighborhood watch?"

Kameo stifled a giggle. "If you did, the crime rate would drop to zero." If possible, he looked gloomier. "Seriously, Salty, what would you like to do, if you could do anything?"

"I can't be a SEAL from nine to five. I don't want to leave for months at a time to go who knows where and maybe never come home. So I have to find something else."

"I hate to sound like a psychiatrist, but have you ever considered doing some aptitude testing to find a profession you'd enjoy?"

Jax winced and sat up, his knees under his chin. "I've done that. They made me a SEAL."

Kameo chuckled. "Well, Salty, if your skills are compatible with being a SEAL, you also have skills compatible with other less dangerous lines of work. Trust me; I'm a professional."

"I saw some ads for a SCUBA diving instructor."

Kameo nodded encouragement. "It's an adjustment, I know, but I also know you. I know you're going to find the perfect second career."

Jax's expression softened as he ran his fingers through her long hair. "I know what I want to do a second time..."

****

Tuesday, October 13

Jax and Kameo's bedside phone rang excruciatingly early. Kameo's hand slammed the receiver off the charger, and she mumbled into it.

"Dr. Rawlings."

An over-deep Scottish brogue pierced her morning. "Is Doctor Adams there?"

Kameo jerked up in bed, suddenly alert. "Brody?"

Jax rolled over, a glare on his face.

"Casey?" The voice on the phone asked.

Kameo wiped the sleep from her eyes. "Yes, Brody. This is Casey. How did you get this number?"

"I sat in your uncle's exam room and claimed every illness in the medical dictionary until he cracked. What time is it there?" His lightheartedness was annoying at this hour.

"Then my next question is, why are you calling me at five in the morning?"

There was a pause. "Five AM? Sorry. I'm really not calling for you, being a married lady, and such. I'm calling about that Bond character you married."

"Really? He can probably hear everything you're saying Brody. Get to it."

Jax wiped both hands down his face and sat on the side of the bed, involved in his usual morning scratching. "What does Mister Hollywood Director want?" As Jax stood and headed to the bathroom, he called out, "Is it about the horses and the runabout we took from the wedding to the ferry? Did anyone reclaim it after we left?"

Hearing Jax in the bathroom, Kameo held out the receiver. "Brody, did you get that, do we owe you for something?"

"No, no. I knew you left the reception. I didn't know you

were honeymooning in Hawaii. I thought we'd have the chance for dinner. You know, take some time to talk about my next film project."

"It's five in the morning."

"My apologies, Casey. I do need to talk to your husband; I have a job for him. If he'd consider it."

Kameo glanced up at Jax, who strode naked back to her bedside and stood hands on hips and quirked his eyebrows questioningly at the phone. She covered the receiver and smirked, "He says he wants to talk to you about a job."

Jax shrugged and scratched at the back of his neck, he whispered, "Can I interview like this?" He shimmied all his body parts at her; she snorted and handed him the phone.

"I'll never tell." She left him for the bathroom, keeping an ear out for the conversation.

"What can I do for you, Brody?"

"You're still a SEAL, right? I mean, you don't lose all that in six weeks, do you?"

"Are you asking as a technicality? Am I being quoted? Is this for the National Intruder?" Jax would never let Brody live that down.

"I deserve that." There was a beat of silence, mutually acknowledging the paparazzi photos of Brody trying to steal a kiss on Kameo's Mackinac Island front porch. "But I need a special forces expert; you are probably that expert. I'm doing a film, and I need your fine-tuning." The silence hung between the three of them. "Did I mention a film credit and a healthy paycheck?"

****

Jax leaned on his elbows over Kameo's laptop as she cooked breakfast. "Have you ever seen a movie script?"

Kameo halted flipping French toast. "Uhh, no."

Jax cocked his head. "Lots of white space on these pages. I guess they use it for notes?" Jax gestured explosions and fighter planes strafing the ground like a kid with model airplanes.

Kameo tossed up two pieces of toast and delivered the plate. "Does it look interesting?"

Jax poured the pureed fruit over the luscious brioche French toast and winked. "At least it's in my skillset."

She arched a brow, poured her tea, and grinned. "Will you take me to the Oscars?"

"Not unless…" They exchanged knowing gazes about their assumed identities and began eating in silence.

****

Kameo and Jax carried their breakfast plates to the sink. With a silent caress and a kiss on the sweet spot behind Kameo's ear, Jax returned to ferreting out errors in Brody Glenn's military blockbuster.

Kameo appreciated the gorgeous view from her kitchen window. "My interview might run for about two hours. I'll text you if it's longer." She ruffled his hair on her way to the bedroom. "Nice hair."

****

Kameo essentially danced into the house with a bag of clinic information in one hand and take-out food in the other. She bellowed, "You home, Salty?" She heard his voice from the patio and was greeted by the dog, sniffing the food bag. "Nothing for you, Doobie. You know you can't eat onions."

Jax sauntered into the kitchen, scratching at his tanned six-pack. "Doobie, this is daddy food. Yours is there." Jax pointed to the metal dog dish. The dog slunk over and pushed it away.

Kameo withdrew a ball on a rope from her purse. "This is

for you, dude." She tossed it through the open doors, and the dog flew by in a blur.

Jax's arms encircled her waist. "Are you a doctor again?" He nosed at her jawline.

She made a face and shook her head. "I've never stopped being a doctor; now I just have a twenty-hour a week job." She unpacked fragrant takeout food and slipped out of her shoes. "How's the script?"

Jax grabbed two sparkling waters from the fridge, and belly laughed. "Brody called me, we talked. He threw down a few more requests. He wants me on set next January. Even offered me a few diving scenes." For a moment, Jax pulled her onto his lap to steal a look at her warm dark eyes.

"I need to remember to tell you how much I love you every day, baby." His lips sealed a kiss on her forehead. "But right now, let's eat." He lifted her back to her feet and picked up his plastic fork. Jax gestured. "I'm not looking forward to meeting the writer, that script borders on fantasy."

With a toss of her ponytail and a smile, Kameo swallowed food. "I think you'd love it out there. All that water and no deadly missions."

He leaned back in the chair, his legs sprawled and shrugged. "Yeah, yeah, yeah. At least it won't be deadly unless I die of boredom."

Chapter 10

LaDonna caught Kirk in an alcove near the locker rooms. She snapped him with her towel as he strolled by. "I have worked up such an appetite, how would you like to follow me home and satisfy that appetite with your prowess?" She purred close to his ear.

Kirk poked at that ear, like an itch he couldn't scratch. "I can't; I have a business meeting tonight."

She pointed a manicured nail at his chest. "Such dedication, that's why you are such a success in every way. How do I get on your calendar?"

Kirk stepped away from LaDonna and nodded, over his shoulder he threw up a hand like a customer forestalling a used car salesperson. "I'll have to get back to you."

Indignation and desire wrestled in her heart. *This would be so much easier if he'd just give in.* "That's fine. Perhaps, I should mix with men my age. They have more stamina."

****

She has thrown down the gauntlet. More stamina? She's not going to find a forty-year-old with my body and skills. Maybe I should introduce her to Wade?

Kirk strolled to the front desk, where Jordan was chatting up a new member for the six-week supersession. As Jordan closed the new member and sent him off with the tee-shirt and tote bag, Kirk moved into Jordan's line of sight.

"Jordie, you are my super sales pro. Nice close." Jordan accepted the compliment while she finished filing the paperwork.

"That's what keeps the doors open." She leaned on her stool and drew a drink from her water bottle. "Whattaya need?" She was always professionally detached at the gym. He could not read her.

"Whatcha doing for dinner tonight?" Kirk watched the sidewalk traffic.

"Oh, big Saturday night. I'm going to a Pedi party with two other widows. We've decided we need foot massages more than men."

Kirk sagged against the counter with a neutral expression. "Have fun with that…" He turned and shook off her statement. *When someone tells you who they are, believe them.*

****

Des moved with different confidence after only a few workouts. He approached Jordan at the desk, smoothie in hand. "Jordan, are there spinning classes I can sign up for?"

"We don't have a class, but if you use that bike in the far corner, you can log on to hundreds of online classes."

"Okay, I'll try that."

"I heard you gave Bobbie tickets to a show. You're a performer?"

"I'm a psychic medium."

"Wow, I've never met one of those."

"Moving to the islands, this is the most I've talked about my gifts ever. I had a close friend in Vegas who was also a psychic, and we shared stories, but he moved. I'm not used to talking about it."

"When did you know you had this ability?"

Des leaned his forearm on the counter and shrugged. "Since I was a kid."

86

Casually, Jordan reached out and laid her hand on his forearm. "Was that frightening to learn you had this ability?"

Des looked straight in her eyes. "Not really." He placed his other hand over hers. "You've been lonely since your husband died, but you need to ask for what you want."

Jordan slid out her hand and crossed her arms over her chest. "I have what I need."

Des shot a finger at her. "But, is it what you want?" He left a show ticket on the counter and nodded politely before he left for the locker rooms.

****

Kirk watched the women's cardio class end and positioned himself at the door. Winded women nodded at him while he shook each of their hands, bolstering them with encouraging words like, "Good form" or "Nice improvement." Until he got to his perennial straggler, LaDonna. He took her hand in both of his and sought her gaze. "My meeting canceled, are you still available for dinner?"

"My invitation wasn't specifically for dinner, but we could eat." She mimicked his over the shoulder, dismissive body language. "Follow me, home?"

Kirk caught his instructor's eye. "It's David's night to close. I'm taking off."

The instructor looked up from his gym bag with a knowing nod.

****

SUNDAY, OCTOBER 18TH

The diner's air conditioner droned as Kirk pushed through the lobby of waiting breakfast customers. Jordan, seated at their usual booth in the corner, moved aside the reserved sign and waved him over.

87

Jordan's raised eyebrow made him suddenly conscious of his wrinkled clothes from yesterday and had him sniffing his less than freshly clothed frame. *I showered, but she caught me and marked me like a cat in heat.*

"Growing a beard?"

Kirk rubbed at his silver bristles. "No, ahh, just an unexpectedly occupied morning."

Jordan looked over her eyeglasses at him. "Oh, Spanish food is back on the menu?"

"I thought our Sunday mornings were supposed to be positive and uplifting."

"The morning after LaDonna's flat tire, you floated in here on a testosterone laced cloud. Has the plumeria lost its scent?"

He grabbed up her coffee mug, gulped, grimaced, and stared into its depths glumly. "I broke my primary rule."

"No fraternizing with gym customers?"

Kirk nodded. "It was a rule for a reason." He tapped his knuckle on the table.

Jordan was relentlessly cheerful. "Because every encounter from now until the end of time will be uncomfortable." Kirk nodded. "Should I put her on the mailing list for Big Kahuna Fitness?" Kirk and Kahuna had an arrangement. Kirk got the gung-ho exercise zealots, and Kahuna took the ladies who lunched and the people who paid their monthly dues and waved as they passed the gym.

Kirk slid back in the booth and drew his fingers through his short hair. "I don't know if even Kahuna can handle her."

"Is that you kissing and telling?"

"You can look at her and recognize she takes high maintenance to a new level."

"And you've done more than look. Twice." Jordan took her mug from his side of the table and raised her hand to the server. The young man nodded and appeared tableside.

"Your usual? Two egg white vegetable omelets, rye toast, no butter, the fruit of the day is pineapple."

Kirk moaned and shook his head. "When isn't it?"

Jordan nodded to the server and then faked sympathy. "Perhaps you need a breakfast with some simple carbs to… you know, replenish energy."

The server grinned. "We've got a great power smoothie. Let me mix one for you, Mr. Roman." He topped off their coffee and was gone.

"Let's take a break from my love life. Let's talk about you, Jordan."

"Simple, I don't have a love life."

"Then let's leave mine alone. How was that Pedi party?"

Jordan smiled charmingly. "You only had to ask. I got the hot stone massage with the gel manicure. It's been a while, but those hot stones, they might just be as good as sex."

Kirk blinked hard and shook his head. "A while? That last man, maybe he wasn't doing it right?"

Jordan flashed jazz hands. "That's why he was the *last* man."

They stirred their coffee in awkward silence. Then Jordan put the clipboard on the table. "Hawaiian News Network is coming out on the twenty-fifth to film healthy treat blurbs for Halloween. I've got the release paperwork for the parents of next week's class."

Kirk poked at the air. "Make sure we have fresh tee-shirts for the staff…"

"We have the Healthy Hawaii shirts in orange, with your logo on the sleeve and back. They are being delivered on

Tuesday. You do have extra clothing and a razor in your office bathroom, right?"

He drew his hand down his face and sighed.

****

MONDAY, OCTOBER 19TH

Kirk walked to the front door at 06:55 as was his custom, shut off the alarm system and unlocked the doors. He was not pleased to see LaDonna, bright and early, in stalking mode. His smile froze. He had to welcome loyal customers. Sadly, LaDonna was a little too loyal.

She petted his forearm as she strutted in. "I'm so happy; I have the entire day to spend here."

Kirk smiled broadly over her head at the rehab class, making their slow way inside. He barely spared a glance at LaDonna. "Excuse me; I need to help these ladies." He bent solicitously toward the two white-haired women from the condos above the gym. They were the only two left using walkers. "Good day, ladies. You're both moving more gracefully this morning."

The women beamed. "I can tell the difference since we've been coming to class." Flora boasted.

"I talked to several of our class members last week. They all said when they started, they were using walkers." Georgia agreed.

Kirk walked between the two of them, one hand on each woman's back, ushering them into the exercise area. "That's right, ladies. You stick with me; I'll have you in the hula class before you know it."

They twittered happily. And another woman passed them on her way in. "You know he will, too."

Kirk waited at the door until all the class members assembled. LaDonna attempted to follow, but he quietly closed the door behind himself. Seeing her standing and scowling through the window, he also closed the privacy blinds. He smiled the smile of an escapee.

****

The boxes in the guest room were understood to be less vitally important that those already unpacked. Jax wandered into the far wing of the house, empty plate in hand. "Babe, where's the Paleo waffles I bought?" He found his wife, head down in a large wardrobe box.

"Have you tasted those things? Even the dog wouldn't eat them."

He walked over to admire her derriere in trim black uniform pants. With a gentle swat on her buttock, he admonished, "Anything this nice needs to be worshiped."

Muffled by dumped clothing fallen off the rod in transit, she barked, "I'd like to cover my ass if I could find my lab coat. Have you seen it?"

"Last time I saw that was Mackinac after I ripped it off you and tossed it to the floor."

"Oh, I forgot about that. I wonder if it got packed? I might have to stop at the uniform shop on the way to work."

"But I'm hungry."

"Oh, poor thing. What does Paleo man do when Paleo woman is leaving for work?"

"Probably what Kirk does, make eggs. He bored me to tears the other morning while we swam, telling me about his vegetable rotation with his early morning eggs."

Kameo tied her long hair up in a scrunchie and poked him in the belly. "If it's Tuesday, it must be tomatoes? Go, catch a fish in your teeth. Impress the tourists. I thought you were going to interview landscapers?"

"Just because you have a real job and I'm flushing out stupid stuff in scripts, don't make fun of me. I can do the landscaping."

"No, no. You'll get tied up on set, and the house will look like a jungle. Find a guy."

"Maybe I'll find a girl?"

She slipped into her Hush Puppies at the door, slung her purse over her shoulder and blew him a kiss. "First day, I don't know how late I'll be. I wouldn't make fun of you ever." She closed the door and was gone.

Jax strolled back to the pristine kitchen. The blender sat in pieces draining after Kameo's morning smoothie. That was his level of commitment, he mused as he tossed the remaining berries into the blender with Almond milk and Chia seeds. As the fruit flew in circles he wondered how many times Brody would call today?

****

In the ladies' locker room, LaDonna dialed the number one restaurant for celebrities and highbrow foodies on the island. Chef Hilo's had recently won five Michelin stars. "May I speak to Chef Hilo?"

"This is Chef George; may I help you?"

"You may help me speak to Chef Hilo." She posed elegantly as if in front of Chef Hilo.

"I'm sorry, he's off the island today. How can I meet your needs?"

"Well, I had my heart set on Chef Hilo." LaDonna fluffed her hair in front of the mirror.

"I'm Chef George. This is *my* restaurant."

LaDonna gave a deep sigh. "I genuinely want to impress my boyfriend, and I urgently need to have lunch cooked for us and delivered today.

"I'll do my best. I do have a certain menu I'm working with today."

"Oh no, I have specific menu needs." She drew a handwritten list from her cleavage.

There was a pregnant pause. "Fine. What do you need?"

"Do you have a pen and paper?"

His voice became increasingly lock-jawed. "Yes. I'm ready."

****

LaDonna clicked off her call with a smug grin and headed out of the ladies' locker room for the reception desk. She tapped a long, acrylic nail on the counter to get the attendant's attention. "Yes, ma'am?" He inquired solicitously.

"I have a special catered lunch coming in at one o'clock, if I happen to be occupied, will you page me overhead?" She flashed her ID card.

"Of course, ma'am."

She wandered to the health bar feeling inordinately pleased with herself. "I'll have that antioxidant smoothie and one of those pistachio biscotti." She passed over her gym card for the charges.

Sitting at the bench in the area, LaDonna sipped her chalky smoothie and waited for what she called 'the old lady class' to end. When Kirk finally opened the doors and gave every participant a personal, encouraging goodbye, she was there with an ingratiating smile for each 'doddering' attendee. She reserved her beaming smile for Kirk.

Kirk nodded at her straight-faced and headed directly for the men's locker room. LaDonna narrowed her eyes. *You can run, but you can't hide.*

****

At one pm sharp, her delivery from Chef Hilo's arrived in insulated bags. LaDonna ripped off a few bills for a gratuity. "I'll return the insulated bags later, is that okay?" She played coy with the driver. He nodded and was gone.

The delicious scents of food wafted behind her as she took the stairs down to Kirk's office. The door was not only closed; it was locked. LaDonna bent at the knees to look up and down through the door's mini blinds. Then she heard his voice from the main gym. That door opened, and participants thronged out to get to the showers. She held the bags aloft to keep the crowd from bouncing the food. Kirk moved within the throng, and as he approached her, she held the bags higher. "Kirk, I've ordered a heavenly lunch for us from Chef Hilo's." The sweaty class members raised their brows at the mention of this famous restaurant. Kirk cut through to stand in front of her.

"I'm sorry, I wish you had asked me before you ordered. I'm booked up straight through the day. I'll have to suck down a protein drink while I teach the next class."

****

Chef Hilo? For Lunch? Good God, that costs a fortune. What does she want from me?

LaDonna put on a major pout. "A body like yours can't go without food."

"That's why I have a protein drink waiting for me upstairs." He wiped a stream of perspiration trickling down the silver hairs on his chest and into the vee on his shirt. "I'm sorry, but Kerri called out sick today. I have to sub."

LaDonna cast an appraising look at the bags. "Well, luckily, all these items will keep. I insist you come for dinner after your long, arduous day."

Kirk's lips drew grimmer, and he weighed his options. *I don't see a way out of this one. At least she doesn't know where I live.* "Sure, what time?" He asked, dully.

She bobbled her shoulders, moving everything God gave her and grinned. "How is seven?"

Kirk's eyes moved upward, right to the left, and then dropped. "Okay."

"Bring your appetite." She coyly flirted as she turned and left.

****

LaDonna strode to the front desk in full ownership mode. "Kirk wants me to deliver this to his home; he said you had the address."

Without thought, the college student tapped a few keys on the keyboard and jotted the oceanside address on a business card. "There ya go." She went back to reading Shape magazine, and LaDonna darted out the door.

Bursting through her front door with the restaurant food, LaDonna yelped. "Come get this." Consuela arrived wide-eyed, dumbstruck. "All of this needs to be refrigerated. Unpack it carefully to preserve its presentation." There was little chatter from Consuela as she saw elegantly plated food. LaDonna barked. "This isn't for us. I am having a guest this evening, and you will stay in your room." The teen's shoulders drooped as she slid the trifles onto the top shelf and closed the refrigerator. She nodded silently and left for her room.

LaDonna shrilled, "Get back here. You need to thoroughly clean my bathroom, change the bed linens, and clean my bedroom." She picked at her manicure for a moment. "The food must be perfect by seven, do you understand?" Consuela nodded mutely and headed to the cabinet with the vacuum and cleaning supplies.

Seated at her computer, LaDonna brought up Kirk's address. "Yes!" She exclaimed when the seaside mansion filled the monitor. Property listings showed it owned by an LLC for the past eighteen years. *My money isn't there.* She keyed in Silver

SEAL Fitness and found the same ownership. So Kirk fell into wealth, at least enough to buy that home and that business eighteen years ago. The tax records showed a healthy value. *He's loaded.*

****

Kirk opened the exercise room door and peeked out. Des, passing toward the men's locker room, laughed. "She's gone. I saw her leave."

Kirk opened the door wider. "The redhead?"

Des nodded and laughed again. "Hey, she's not after me, and I'm still nervous around her. Something about her is…"

"Over the top? Too hot to handle?"

The two men clapped a high five, and Des grasped Kirk's hand. "Seriously, you want to steer clear of this one." Kirk's gaze darkened at the suggestion.

"Is this your Spidey sense or just man to man advice?"

Des shrugged. "Maybe some of both. I'd steer clear of her if I were you."

Chapter 11

Consuela frowned in frustration. LaDonna did not seem disposed to leave home this afternoon. That would mean endless housework, no American TV, or any precious time on the computer. Consuela was arduously teaching herself English between television, junk mail, and the computer. One bad girl at the convent showed her how to erase the browsing history on a search engine, and that was golden information.

Each trip to the grocer, she secreted singles and change into an envelope under a plastic sheet in her bird's cage. LaDonna, who frequently went through her things, would never look there. Consuela was determined. As soon as she knew enough English and had a few of the bills with the number twenty on them, she would head to the Mexican consulate on King Avenue.

Consuela knew she had bits and pieces of valuable information about a woman named Isabel Huerta, information that surely would earn her freedom.

****

At eight minutes after seven, Kirk dropped the heavy door knocker once. He counted, hoping for no answer, and then heard LaDonna's grating Spanish admonition. "Get in your room and stay there."

That piqued his curiosity, he wouldn't talk to a dog like that, and he thought LaDonna lived alone. *Oh, please, not a threesome.* He shifted his jean's pockets and situated himself from the Harley ride over.

LaDonna swept open the door, oozing graceful sensuality. The scent of ten thousand jasmine flowers along with twenty-eight dozen roses smacked Kirk in the nose. *How many spritzes of Joy did she pump?* He immediately thought of his long-dead mother.

She posed at the open door, wearing a drop shoulder knit top molded to her curves. Her waist was next to nothing with the deep teal belt cinched tight. Her hips showed off her dangerous curves in a pair of mostly spandex crop pants. She was barefoot, wearing foot jewelry. Her riotous red hair was growing out and curling around her face and neck. "Good evening," she purred as she gestured him in.

Oh, God, I am on the menu. Des was right. Don't be such a big crybaby; Dave hasn't been laid in months. I should give her his number.

As they moved through the living room, LaDonna nearly hip-bumped him, whispering in his ear. "Do you need to shower?"

Kirk sniffed his polo. "I think I'm good. I'm not good?" He threw out both hands and turned a slow circle.

"You look divine from here… follow me."

"We're eating in the bedroom?" He scratched at his neck as he followed her.

"The last time you were here, my suite was not set up." She coaxed him into the room. "See my television and this elegant sitting area?" She posed at her chair and gestured to his across the small table. A standing champagne chiller stood between them.

Kirk held out her chair. "Would you like me to open the champagne?" Kirk read the label and stopped at Taittinger because this bottle was more than two c-notes at his wine shop.

"While you're pouring, I'll get our first course." She rolled a tea cart to the table and placed the iced crystal tray of eight of the fattest oysters he'd ever seen.

"Are they all for me? Won't you join me?"

She flirted over her champagne flute. "They're all for you, my dear."

I am on the menu. Great, eight giant shells of mucous. "Is there any horseradish?" *It's the only thing that will banish the slime.* She obligingly reached for the cut crystal jar with the silver spoon.

He felt like an offering to Jabba the Hutt as he slathered horseradish over the oyster and swallowed it whole. He felt the burn all the way down to his belly. *Is this thing quivering inside me?*

LaDonna took absolute joy in his devouring the mollusk. "Good?"

He nodded his head, tight-lipped. "Umhum." *Seven more to go, I'm glad one of us is enjoying it.* When Kirk reached for the last and largest oyster, the spoon in the jar rattled. "Are you out of horseradish?" LaDonna shrugged. "Have any seafood sauce?" She shook her head no. "Taco sauce?" Again, negative. "Are you sure I can't share this last one?"

"I don't really care for them; I adore watching my lovers eat them." She sat back in the chair and poured more bubbly for them, smiling triumphantly.

Kirk pushed the chilled platter back. *Do I dare wash this one down with champagne?* "It looks like you have quite a bit of food this evening. I better save this one."

LaDonna cast shade as she rose and returned with the chilled avocado salad, and bright red onion sliced thinly over the mixed greens.

"Ooh, this looks yummy." He waited until they could start

together, and he paced himself. His tongue swept over his teeth, trying to get the horseradish from between them. His belly felt scorched. There was an uncomfortable silence through the salad course, and his stomach growled in protest.

LaDonna removed the domed cover from an exquisite looking petit quiche. She cut it in half and served him. As she sat and prepared to eat, she began her third degree. "You seem like you're all alone on the island." He chewed and shrugged. "Do you have a family?" He shook his head. "How can it be a man like you isn't married?"

He swallowed and thought about the worst possible answers he could give her. Certainly, something from his past would end the inquisition.

He put down his fork and dried his palms on the napkin on his lap. "I used to be married." LaDonna cocked her head like a Bichon Frise. "She died." He watched her throat close-mid swallow.

"Oh, I'm so sorry. How did she die?"

"A wood-chipper accident." *Keep digging, honey. Nobody needs to know my story.* He resumed eating, and after a swallow, he nodded to her. "Ever been married?"

She looked away and then looked back at Kirk, her dark eyes wide. "I was very young. He was much older. He died."

Kirk raised his glass and wiggled his brows. "We're really bad for people, aren't we?"

She drew back in affront. "He was *very* old." She was quiet for a beat. "Any children?"

He finished his quiche and nodded. "A son. We lost contact decades ago. I always wanted a daughter." *Now for the home run.* "Have you thought about having kids? We'd make a beautiful daughter."

She pushed back her plate and posed, her hand fluffing the hair at her neck. "I'm not mother material. Was he a problem child?" She sat back, crossed one long leg over the other, and scrutinized him through her dark eyelashes.

"How bad can a kid be? If only he knew how to work a wood-chipper." Kirk dabbed at his lips with his cloth napkin. "But Mom came to his rescue, then…"

LaDonna rose and cleared his plate. While her back was to him, he smelled his breath. *Horseradish, onions, garlic, and eggs. I want a toothbrush.*

She returned to the table after a trip to the small refrigerator next to the suite's bar. She held two crystal compote dishes as she wiggled back to the table. Kirk squinted at the green and brown concoction topped with whipped crème.

"Whatcha got there, missy?" He reared back on two legs of the chair. Pistachio nuts topped the whipped crème. "Pistachio pound cake?"

"Yes, mixed with chocolate mousse. Isn't it divine?"

It's not the worst thing I've eaten tonight. "What a nice ending to the evening."

She sat, barely touching her dessert. "Oh but wait. There are more adventures to come." She disappeared behind a wall in the direction of her bathroom. Kirk heard fabric rustling and the occasional soft grunt.

Kirk checked his watch. *Seven fifty. Jeeze, I've been there all night.*

"I've chosen a stirring film for us to watch. It's brief." She spoke from behind the wall. "I have a robe for you in the other room if you'd care to be more comfortable."

He looked at the broad king-sized bed with scores of pillows and a new fluffy duvet cover, turned down. "I'm good."

She appeared wearing a diaphanous caftan, bells at her wrists and ankles. *Is that a belly dancer's costume under there?*

She led him to the couch in front of her bed. "Let me get this started." She looked over her shoulder. "Do you like Middle Eastern music?"

"I heard my share of it the military… got anything else?"

She flipped through the DVD menu. All of the titles were suspiciously convoluted. He read Ten Best Belly Dancing Songs. Yearning, Shik, Shak, Shok, Habibi Yah Einy, Hopa Tito Balala, and Desert Storm Original Mix. He remembered Desert Storm; *it wasn't like this. She is bonkers. I have got to get out of here.* He checked his watch again. "I only have about another fifteen minutes."

"Oh, these are short songs…" She turned to him on the couch and assumed a classical belly dancer's stance. The drums began, and he reflexively covered his Harley belt buckle with both hands.

Veiled, she was exquisite. He saw brilliant red lipstick under the sheer blood-red chiffon. Her long fingers worked the brass zills in her palms, supplementing the visceral sound of the film's stringed instruments and drums. She shimmied closer to Kirk's knee and turned, artfully bending backward, not quite into his lap. The brass bells on her wrist skimmed his fly, and Kirk straightened out his legs for relief.

She whipped her head as if she'd done this with a long full head of hair. While Kirk watched her back and shoulders undulating up and down, her caftan dropped to the floor, and she artfully kicked it away. Those deadly hips of hers whipped the tribal belt of heavy coins and tassels at Kirk, in full sexual assault. Her sheer harem pants split on the outer edge gave him a front-row seat to the well-toned legs he usually saw under spandex.

Eight minutes into the DVD, Kirk noticed the musicians deep into their siren's songs and the trio of dancing women who couldn't carry LaDonna's coin belt. As the steady drumbeat quickened, LaDonna spun, eyes closed. *If I sneak out, would she notice?*

Twelve minutes into the video Kirk recollected the only thing worse than rejecting his personal belly dancer would be if that DVD had been porn. Something like Forrest Hump was far from personal. Having a woman dancing so artistically in the privacy of a boudoir should have been every man's dream. Kirk watched the timer in the lower corner of the flat-screen television. He was seconds away from dealing with her 'offering'.

As the music rhythmically slowed, the piper began a song that should raise a cobra. She dropped to her knees before Kirk and bent backward, shimmying body parts that astounded him. LaDonna's hands made lazy circles at her wrists above her head and raised to one knee to slide into a split. On the polished wooden floors, she swung her back leg around and spun on the cheeks of her fine ass. Her coin belt spun off with her voluminous harem pants, leaving her in a jeweled G-string and bra. Now, beneath him, she was as sinuous as a cobra, her hips moving opposite her shoulders, rippling her tight belly. Rising to her knees, so close he inhaled her heated pheromones, her bra coins dashed against his knees. As the music came to a riotous end, she threw her face into his lap, her hands clutching his belt buckle.

To the sound of her deep breathing and his gasp, he bolted to his feet, throwing her hands off him, nearly rolling her away on the floor. "I'm very sorry, but as I said earlier, I'm pressed for time." She grabbed his hands, and he worked out of her grasp. "I've got to get going."

"If you feel you must, you must." She pouted, her dark eyes turning on the waterworks.

Kirk raised her chin with a finger and gave her a grim look. "It really was a good dinner. You dance … so… beautifully, you're wasting your talents on a guy like me… I told you I couldn't stay." He stepped back from her. "Do you want me to show myself out?"

By now, LaDonna retrieved the pieces and parts of her tribal dancewear. "I'll walk you out." She raised a defiant chin at the front door. "I'll call Benny at Kahuna's. He'd die to spend this time with me."

Kirk nodded agreeably as he strode to his bike. Before he mounted his Harley, he turned back. "You do that. He gets off on this stuff." Kirk waved his hand toward her bedroom. "Have a nice night." He expected a potted plant off the back of his helmet as he started up and rode away.

Stupid, stupid man. Kirk realized he'd lived in that mansion like a monk if monks lived with saunas, Jacuzzis, and convection ovens, overlooking the ocean. *I am so wrapped up in cutting women out of my life, it doesn't surprise me, I fell prey to a temptress. Twice is enough.* Tonight, it took every bit of self-control to keep from pulling her lyrical hips between his knees and devouring her from breasts to her dangerous delta.

All this time, he'd been afraid of Jordan. He treated her with deferential space. *She's my right hand at the gym.* I've been jealous of the way the new men look at her. It's not just because she's a merry widow with a full life. *But she never mentions wanting men. She was married. He died. I probably couldn't measure up to the guy who left Jordan sitting pretty. I want to move forward. Seeing Jax happy, I want to be happy.* Kirk gunned the engine and gritted his teeth.

CHAPTER 12

He eschewed his jacket in an effort to cool off in the twenty-minute ride from Diamond Head to Kapiolani Boulevard, where Jordan's condo overlooked the canal. It was kind of late for a casual call, but they'd been friends for eighteen years, surely she wouldn't mind. He'd expected the refreshing breeze to dash his ardor, but he felt more revved up now than when he'd started. *Must be the damn oysters.*

He pulled up to the gate and spoke to the anonymous voice in the box. "Kirk Roman to see Jordan Perry in 2918."

"Is she expecting you?"

"No."

"Please park in the temporary parking space and come to the front desk. I'll contact Ms. Perry."

Kirk followed the direction and then strode up to the marble counter and, hands-on-hips looking windblown, waited for permission to enter the inner sanctum.

The muscular young security guard stood up from a stack of police academy notebooks. "Ms. Perry says you may go on up."

****

In all the years she'd known him, Kirk had only been to her condo once when she had gallbladder surgery. She couldn't imagine the reason for this visit. *Did somebody die?* She decided even if someone was dead, she wasn't going to greet him in her chenille robe with the chili dog stains on it. She ran to the closet, pulled out her prettiest caftan with purple flowers, pinched her cheeks, and fluffed her hair.

She counted to ten before she answered his knock. "Hi. What a surprise. Is everything okay?"

"No. Everything is not okay."

She wrung her hands as she ushered him into the living room. "What is it? Is someone dead?"

He gave her an exasperated look. "You don't have a belly dancer get-up under that thing, do you?"

Her eyes went wide. "Have you been drinking?"

"Only a glass of champagne."

"Does champagne make you…" She searched for the word, "goofy?"

"You don't understand. I just came from a dinner with a surprise belly dancer."

"Ooh. Do you have anything to confess, Mr. Roman? Because we don't do confessions on Mondays. They're Saturdays before the six o'clock mass."

"No. I just need normalcy."

"You silver-tongued devil. You really know how to sweep a girl off her feet."

Kirk scrubbed a hand through his hair. "No, you don't understand." To Jordan's complete shock, he picked up her hand and kissed her palm. "Normalcy is great. I hope we're on the same page about it when I say, 'I wanna be normal with you'."

Jordan cocked her head, and gingerly pulled her hand away. "Let's sit down. Normalcy is great as long as it makes your heart beat a little faster. I mean, you can't live in Disneyland, can you?"

Kirk paced out to the lanai and leaned on the wall, looking up and down across the canal to the row of hotels on Waikiki. "You've been right about so many things."

"O…kay…"

"I'm an asshole. I mean, you're an incredible woman. You inspire me. You're one of the bravest people I know. I mean, look how you've transformed your life…"

"Thank you? Don't you wanna sit down, Kirk? You want some water?"

"You've shared your refreshing perspective with people, and you truly make a difference." Jordan walked out to join him on the lanai, seeing he wasn't able to settle yet. He took her hand. "You look so beautiful with the breeze blowing through your hair."

Jordan tilted her head. "See, these are things you've never said to me before, so I'm having a little trouble keeping up…"

"I said I was an asshole." He looked at her from under his lashes. Her silver hair blew across her face, and he gently pushed it back with two fingers. "I wonder if I'm too much of an idiot for you to work your magic on me?"

"I…uh…" *I need to ask for what I want, or the Universe will never give it to me.*

"Will you let me break rule number two?"

Jordan's heart thudded. "Never get involved with gym employees?"

"You've been with me since the beginning, Jordie. We can break the rules if we want to."

She stepped into his space and let him wrap arms around her to draw her closer. They were strong arms, and they felt phenomenal. Was it the years of denying this that made them feel so divine? Everything in her fought against good sense. She ran a gentle hand down the side of his face. "I'm not quite sure what happened to you tonight. And I want to accept your invitation to break rule number two. I also think we need a little cooling off period. If this isn't just impulse, it will keep till tomorrow night. Would you like to come over for dinner and a movie?"

Kirk groaned. "No belly dancing? No oysters? No pistachios, no garlic, no onions?"

She shook her head. "There's a story there I don't want to know. Poké bowls, action-adventure movie, normalcy at seven?"

He sighed. "Sounds great." His head lowered for a quick kiss and a bear hug.

Chapter 13

Before the front doors opened, Kirk handed Jordan his cellphone. "Would you record a pleasant but direct greeting on this. I need you to be explicit that I can only return calls between classes and until seven at night."

Jordan buried a chuckle. "Is this your new company cellphone?"

"Yeah, whatever, you'll do a nicer job than I will right now." Kirk was visibly irked.

Jordan watched him turn on his megawatt smile as he unlocked the door for the television camera crew.

By nine in the morning, Hurricane LaDonna blew in. She dropped her Louis Vuitton purse on the counter and dug out her phone. "Why am I being directed to Kirk's company phone?"

Jordan smiled sweetly. "What number did you dial, Ms. Garza-Mendoza?" The irate woman pressed her recent calls button and held it up for viewing. "Oh, that's Kirk's number, he's bombarded with calls, and he wanted to channel them in a different direction."

"I don't appreciate being 'channeled' as you say. I need to see Kirk immediately."

Jordan looked up at the monitor showing the filming in the main gym. "I'm afraid he won't be available immediately. He'll be tied up for at least another hour. Didn't you get the email about the canceled classes this morning?"

"This has nothing to do with class."

"Obviously."

"What?" LaDonna growled.

It's not about class. Jordan offered, "I'm sorry, the boutique is closed today."

"I don't want anything from the boutique." LaDonna smacked her palm on the counter. The pencil cup jumped. Jordan did not. "I need Kirk."

Jordan nodded slightly. *Don't we all?* In the most syrupy and irritating tone Jordan could conjure, she leaned toward LaDonna. "I hear you saying you feel the need to speak with Kirk. Sadly," she gestured to the monitor on the wall, "he's taping now and will be unavailable until after eleven."

LaDonna surveyed the gym lobby, and seeing no one, stormed toward the main gym. Jordan pressed the button, and the swinging doors to that area locked with a firm click. LaDonna hit the doors and bounced off them. With a yelp and squeal, she stood with her hands on hips and slowly turned to Jordan. Through gritted teeth she ground out, "He'll be free at eleven?"

Jordan nodded. "After eleven."

"Fine." LaDonna stomped to the main door. "I'll be back after eleven."

* * * *

LaDonna Garza-Mendoza experienced frustration as an assault upon her person. She was unfamiliar with the concept of 'wait' and 'tolerate'. In her prior persona as Isabel Huerta, people waited on and for her. She got what she wanted when she wanted it. She felt bruised; she felt dismissed; she felt devalued. *This will not stand.*

As she drove down Piikoi Street, a flyer slid off the car seat and caught her attention at the traffic light. A service called "Steamy Yoni" promised immeasurable benefits, physical, emotional, and spiritual. This was a gift from heaven. She pulled into an empty parking spot and dialed the number.

"Steamy Yoni, this is Arwen, how may we heal you?" A sincere voice greeted LaDonna who immediately turned on her charm.

She ground her molars, using the voice she saved for nuns and priests. "Arwen, good morning. I want to make an appointment."

"Have you visited us before?"

"No. I have an immediate need for cleansing."

There was momentary silence and the sound of a keyboard. "I regret our nine thirty sessions are preparing right now. I couldn't take you until eleven."

An aggravated groan escaped LaDonna's lips. "What if I offered to pay for your current guests to move to the eleven o'clock hour, and I bought all of your current studio time at triple the rate? I crave privacy."

There was silence on the line.

"Arwen, are you there, dear?"

The receptionist stumbled over her words, and there was an indecipherable chatter in the background. "Would you like to hold these reservations with a credit card?"

LaDonna smiled in satisfaction, feeling a surge of relief. She rattled off her black Amex card number and patiently drove the few blocks to Steamy Yoni.

Somehow LaDonna expected more exotic ambiance than a series of gauzy draperies in a flat above a card store and scooter rental shop. Still, she was desperate in her own way and open to anything that promised relief. The low tones of ocean waves played from hidden speakers. Candles protected by tall glass cylinders flickered, emitting the fragrances of lavender, lemon, and bergamot.

Arwen introduced her to Wave, the proprietress, who guided her down a hall to a dressing room. "I'm so grateful you were led to our healing energies today. After you've removed your clothes and are wearing only your yoni gown, I'll meet you in the next room to discuss your medical history and your emotional and spiritual needs."

****

LaDonna flew down the stairs, talking to herself, impatiently clicking her car's remote. It was unlocked and running by the time her fingers touched the handle. *What the hell did they blow up my hoohoo? Relaxation, my ass. Right now, I would screw the pirates of the Caribbean.* The color of her yoni gown did nothing to relax her, even though it was as placid as the deepest blue Mexican ocean. *That weirdo Wave suggested "spring flower petals for a relaxing uplift."*

Wave promised a vaginal reawakening. She dropped chamomile into the pot and mentioned something about treating anxiety.

LaDonna plopped into the warm car seat and squirmed, flipping the dial to open the car's roof. *What kind of opposite reaction is this? Damn Kirk Roman. Damn him.*

****

What was up with Tuesday morning traffic? Did every department store have a sale? LaDonna didn't consider closing the convertible top as she swung into the parking garage. Kirk's prized motorcycle was parked right next to the stairs. She caught her purse and turned to march into the fitness center when she ran

112

into a broad chest covered with a leather jacket. Both of them were rushing, heads down, determined to make their destination.

"Oops." She stared up at his fiercely cobalt blue gaze. "Going somewhere, Kirk?" She tapped her watch. "Your toady said you'd be available after eleven. It's ten fifty-five."

****

Kirk stepped back and hooked his thumbs in his back pockets. With a sweeping gaze, he arched a brow and expelled a deep breath. "You're not going to be happy with me, LaDonna."

With the flats of her palms, she pushed him back. "I'm not happy with you now. You screen my calls; you don't return them. What am I to think? You avoid my classes; you've deferred my one-on-ones to your assistant. And I danced for you."

"That's right. I have done every one of those things. It's because I broke my own rule when you bewitched me."

"Bewitched you!" She dropped her purse and threw up both hands.

"My dear, you are a rare gem of a woman. It's positively invigorating to believe you would find me, a man my age, attractive."

She stood stunned, and he held his next statement. *Here she blows.* "LaDonna, I cannot date you. It's a rule I laid down when I opened this fitness center. It's just wrong."

She stomped. "Wrong is leading me on. I took you into my bed not once but twice, and this is how you end us?"

"Honey, there was no us. What we had was naked gymnastics. I can't do that. I was wrong."

"I guess confessing your sins makes you think you're absolved." She waved her hand between them.

"I'm trying to right my wrong the best way I know."

113

She tossed her head back and laughed. "No wonder you don't speak to your son. No wonder he doesn't let you know where he is. You are coldly cruel, Kirk Roman. You do not deserve me." She waved her index finger under his nose.

"You pegged me. You're right. You should walk away and never look back. I'll cancel your membership and refund your fees. No harm, no foul."

"It's never about the money. It's always about the heart."

Kirk silently nodded and waited for her to turn and leave before he threw a long leg over his motorcycle and drove off in the opposite direction.

****

Livid and further sexually keyed up, LaDonna drove into the Ala Moana Center's multi-level parking garage and sought the closest parking space to the bar.

She needed something to calm her nerves. There it was, one of those tourist traps with the umbrella drinks. She saw the bottles of bourbon and shimmed onto the barstool. Handsome and eager to please, the young bartender smiled. "What can I get you today? A mai-tai? It's out signature drink."

"I need something nuanced, something to sip."

"Ahh, I have a 1920 Prohibition style Bourbon…"

"Fine. A shot, make it a double."

She sat, nursing the complex flavors of the drink, watching the Tuesday morning shoppers heading toward the tony shops.

Feeling the bartender's scrutiny, she downed the shot and waved him back. "How about one of those Lychee Mai Tais?"

He nodded professionally and within a few moments returned with a gorgeous drink.

"Do I take a photo or drink it?" She handed him cash to cover the drinks. "I'm going to go sit over there." She pointed to a discrete corner.

He went to make change and she waved him off. He nodded. "Enjoy your privacy."

LaDonna felt the effects of the liquor spreading languid heat through her body. Kirk Roman was the one man she could not control. *He's upset because he broke a rule? The first rule of a con game is don't fall for your mark.* At that, she had to admit, she failed miserably. Was all this groveling worth thirty-nine million?

Every time she felt he was a scintilla away from submission, Kirk would cut and run. Then she had to lure him from further away. Damn his discipline. What must she do to break through that hard shell? She played the lady in need and he happily changed her tire and more. She played the jealousy card and he took that bait. She played the siren and that repulsed him. *Clearly Kirk needs a damsel in distress.*

Chapter 14

She exited the mall and stealthily sought an area without surveillance cameras. When she found a deserted length of concrete wall, she ripped at the back of her gossamer blouse and tossed her emptied wallet over the half wall. When she flung the contents of her purse, everything bounced along the dirty pavement. With final resolution she backed close to the wall, screwed up her courage, and smacked her head on the rough concrete. It was enough force to split her scalp and bathe herself in blood.

Warm viscous fluid trailed down her neck as she staggered toward her car and her audience. "Help, help me." She moaned weakly. "Help me, please." She feigned unconsciousness and collapsed in the aisle near her car. She remained 'unresponsive' until the paramedics arrived. Then, she dazedly recounted an attack.

****

At home Kirk dug through his massive refrigerator, looking for lunch in all the wrong places. *Should have stopped at Agu for ramen on the way home.* He withdrew the egg carton and veggies to rustle up an omelet. *I have to get more creative.* Lighting the burner under the pan, he jumped at the vibration in his back pocket.

The phone displayed 'Hospital'. "Kirk Roman."

"Mr. Roman, this is Kings Medical Center. Your name is the ICE contact for a patient who was just brought in."

"Who is it?" Kirk turned off the burner and leaned against the kitchen island.

"LaDonna Garza-Mendoza."

"Son of a bitch, is it bad?"

"You'll have to speak to the doctor when you arrive. She's in emergency room five."

"Did you ask her about calling me?" Kirk responded hesitantly.

The clerk was impersonal. "I'm afraid she's not able to answer questions at this time. When can we expect you to arrive?"

Kirk drew in a deep breath. "I'll be there in thirty or so." He closed the call and drained a bottle of water before he dialed Jordan. "Hey…"

"What are you up to?" Jordan's sunny smile traveled through the phone line.

"I just got a hinky call from Kings Hospital. Can you get Annie to sit at the front for a couple of hours?"

Jordan's tone sagged. "Am I being fired?"

"That's right. I'm firing you for a couple of hours… I need a witness."

"You need a witness? Does this involve a crime?"

"Yeah. The prima donna intercepted me in our garage, and we had a tiff. I sent her packing, and now she's in the ER, and I'm in her phone as her ICE contact."

The sunshine drained from Jordan's voice. "Oh, yeah, you do need a witness and maybe an alibi. Meet you outside the ER."

On his ride over, Kirk juggled all the permutations of LaDonna's confrontation. She put hands on him, but he never touched her. When he drew the bike to a stop at traffic signals, he looked and felt for scratches.

Why does innocence feel so tenuous with LaDonna? It could be perfectly legit; he chided himself. *What if the poor woman had a car accident? When did I become so paranoid?*

****

Oahu is a vacation destination, and the ER was hopping. A lively tourist town always produced unexpected food allergies from exotic restaurants and dislocated shoulders from newbie surfing accidents. Then there were the dreaded heart attacks when men spent time with ladies by the hour in luxury hotels far from home. In bed three, the Portuguese man o' war sting scared the mother as much as it frightened the twelve-year-old boy. And then there was LaDonna.

Kirk stood on the other side of her curtain, listening to the occupant of the bed breathe. *That is some agonal breathing.* His SEAL training flooded back in an avalanche of battlefield experiences. Someone breathing like that was on the verge of death, yet no one here seemed the least bit concerned. When he gave LaDonna's name, the nurse rolled her eyes, pointed, "Curtain five," and ran.

He peeked around the curtain, and LaDonna lay supine, arms crossed over her chest, sheet up to her chin. Her face was smooth, no frown lines, no grimace of pain. She gasped labored breaths that were totally incongruous to her condition. He read the heart monitor. *Good numbers.* She was pink. He lifted the sheet and pressed her toenail bed, *good capillary refill.* He stood staring as she kept up this unconscious act. He waited; arms crossed over his chest at the head of her bed. No response.

"LaDonna." No retort. A bit louder and more firmly. Silence. *Time for a sternal rub.* He coiled his fingers so his knuckles rested on her sternum and gave her a brisk rub.

Her body bolted upright with a yelp. Kirk recognized the Spanish words, something about 'your mother has balls'.

She clutched at her breasts. "Why did you do that?"

Kirk bent over; his hands clasped behind him. "You weren't responding. It's just a little technique leftover from my SEAL days."

She fought to pull herself together. "What are you doing here?"

"That was sort of my question. They called me and told me I was your in case of emergency contact."

She played pathetic. "I was attacked."

"You look pretty good. No bruises, no abrasions, just a scalp laceration. A couple of stitches, you won't know it happened."

Downcast, her voice was a whisper. "But the trauma from being attacked…"

"It's a good thing you took the self-defense class. Wonder what he looks like?"

"My back will be terribly bruised; he got me from behind."

"Well, you look like you've snapped right back, so let's call a cab and get you home."

Her brows knit. "I can't be alone tonight."

"I've already had them call a service. You won't be alone."

"Can't you stay?"

"We've had that conversation."

"I don't want a stranger taking care of me."

"They won't be a stranger. Think of them as a medical professional. Besides, the SEAL medicine I practice is for the nearly dead."

She pouted. "Fine."

"Have the police taken your statement?"

"I told them I didn't feel well; she said I could go to the station tomorrow."

Kirk clapped his hands and pulled back the curtain facing the nurse's station. "Have you got discharge papers for Ms. Garza-Mendoza?"

****

Kirk pulled his sunnies from his shirt pocket and smiled at Jordan. "I owe you a meal, and I haven't even had lunch yet. Thanks for having my back. How about we cut out early, play hooky at a beach bar and have an early dinner out. We can head to your place for the movie?"

"Is this normalcy?" She batted her eyelashes at him.

"Quasi. The way this day started? What's normal?"

Jordan unlocked her car. "Follow me home, and we can walk to the beach."

"Sure." He winked at her.

"Tonight is going to be my cheat meal, and it's going to count. I'm eating dessert, too."

Kirk shook his head and patted his washboard abs. "I guess I'll let myself go tonight, too."

"Damn straight. If I'm going to work out six days a week, I might as well celebrate on the seventh."

Chapter 15

"Hiya, Hailey!" Kirk waved to the server as he strode to his usual table closest to the deck railing. Kirk enjoyed sunsets best over a plate of tasty food. "So, Jordan, what sounds yummy? Kalua Pig Quesadilla, Spicy Ahi Poké Bowl, Coconut Shrimp, and finish with that twenty-layer cake thing… What's that called, Hailey?"

The server smiled as she wrote things down. "Haupia Crepe Cake. Okay, Chief, how's your Tuesday? Ready for cocktails?" She cocked her hip, and her thick ponytail flipped from one side to the next. She pointed her pen at Jordan. "It's been a while since you've been in, you look great."

Jordan looked at the young server's casual shorts, peasant top, and perennial tan. "Thanks. I'll have one of those mai-tais. Make it a big one."

Hailey scampered away for their drinks, and Jordan leaned conspiratorially to Kirk. "How many women do you bring here? I've never been here, looking good, bad, or otherwise."

Kirk got comfortable in the chair, and his head fell back in laughter. "It is my go-to outdoor place. But seriously, I don't … much …"

"Seriously? Because I've seen you around all kinds of beautiful women for years and you've never noticed one of them. Then you caught the Spanish Flu."

"She's the kind of woman… Yeah, she is kinda like the flu. She came in, and I was stricken. But the fever has broken."

Jordan's grin widened. "You could take up origami."

Kirk rubbed at his jaw and thought on that. "Paper cuts can kill."

Jordan spread her napkin over her lap. "That woman looked like she was ready to kill you this morning." Kirk shrugged. "I hear Heart playing the opening riff to Barracuda every time I see her. What was your attraction to her? You like the danger?"

"I would call it hit and run. She kept hitting, and I ran."

Jordan shook her head. "But it's so out of character for you." Her voice softened. "You have no idea how much you surprised me last night. You were all I could think of all night." Kirk's gaze scanned the near-empty deck bar. Her voice dropped to a whisper. "Your mid-evening arrival was unexpected."

There was a beat of silence as waves played on the shore, and the breeze swept the palms. The sun ducked behind fluffy white clouds when Kirk admitted. "Maybe this is how I used to be before my life fell apart."

"I know a lot about life falling apart…"

"Not like mine. In fact, I can't believe we haven't had this talk before. After dessert, you may not want to sit with me in the dark."

Jordan stopped spinning her rose gold waterfall ring, and her hands dropped to her lap. "Are you trying to scare me before dessert? Because unless you're a werewolf, I'm eating dessert. If you morph in the middle of dinner, I'll take it to go."

Kirk threw back his head as his hands clawed, and he howled, engendering stares from the other diners.

"I've known you for eighteen years." She lowered her voice and bent closer. "I know you've been to prison."

"But you don't know the whole story." Kirk thoughtfully focused on the dinner knife beside his plate. His left hand smoothed the large napkin on his lap, and he drew in a long breath.

"I'm listening if you want to tell me."

"The day of the accident I wasn't driving, but I said I was. My wife was driving. She was crazy upset with me because while we were at a couple's retreat, she asked me for a divorce. I asked her, wasn't staying together the point of coming to this out of the way resort for a weekend of counseling?"

Jordan nodded thoughtfully. "That's rough."

"She was determined to be done with my military career. According to her I was an absentee husband and worse than no husband at all."

"Some women can't handle the separation. You never mentioned being divorced."

"We never got that far. I should have insisted on driving, but it was her car. Take one winding country road, one unstable woman wanting to restart a worn-out argument and a kid running after a dog. You get a tragedy." Kirk ended his confession as their drinks arrived. Once their server was gone, he raised his glass. "To honesty."

"But if she was driving, why did you…"

"The whole thing should have been called a tragic accident. We were out in the boonies; there was a good old boy sheriff, we were in a fancy sports car. I was trying to protect her; God knew where they would hold her if they took her in. I knew my son needed his mother."

"Your son?"

"This good old boy walked toward us, cuffs out. I stepped up; I wouldn't let him take her away. I figured I'm a Navy SEAL; I'll have the weight of the Navy behind me. It didn't work out that way."

"Oh, God. What happened to your wife and son?"

"I told you she was unstable. While I was in prison, my son was at an away game. Time alone with her thoughts… she committed suicide."

Jordan's eyes were damp with unshed tears, and she gently put her hands over his balled fists. The server broke into the moment.

"Our kitchen is a little backed up. I'm sorry, may I get you another round of drinks on the house while you're waiting?"

Kirk softly threaded his fingers into Jordan's and smiled at the server. "Sure."

"You've never mentioned a son. What happened to him?"

"He lived with my sister in his last two years of high school. He'd been raised with me in the Navy. He graduated high school early and went straight into a college with an ROTC program. Hard to believe he became a SEAL, too." Kirk slid out of her hands, and he raised his glass to his lips. "Losing contact with him has been my greatest enduring loss."

Jordan sucked down the first mai-tai and dove into the next one wide-eyed.

Kirk laughed and put a hand on her drinking arm. "I don't want to carry you home, slow down."

"So, you were in jail for four years for a crime you did not commit?"

Kirk shook his head. "Good behavior got me out in less than three years. Then there was the riot…"

Jordan pushed back in her chair. "Riot?" She looked around for a response to her squeal.

"Yeah, there was a prison riot. I pulled a guard into the infirmary; I knew he was a target. I kept the guard, the doctor, and a nurse hidden. I protected the patients in the beds." He drew on his straw and shrugged. "Kind of an unstable situation."

"Yah think?" Jordan picked up her water glass and guzzled half of it.

Kirk shrugged again. "Hey, it wasn't my first siege. When I came up for parole, I found out I had a new lawyer. Turns out, one of the prisoners, a kid who was going through heroin withdrawal, was one of the men in the infirmary. I took him under my wing. Got him eating better, kept him exercising, and away from his old friends. Apparently, he had a grateful father, who was a major software inventor. When the boy got out of prison looking and feeling better than ever, Evan told me if I could do it for his son, I could do it for a living."

"So, it's Silver SEAL because of Evan Silver? *The* Evan Silver?"

Kirk chuckled. "I wasn't this silver when you met me, was I?"

She shrugged. "No, and I was a redhead…"

"So now you know everything. Are we eating dessert here?"

"You're not shaking me that easy, Roman. I've invested eighteen years of friendship."

"So, what's the movie tonight?" Hailey delivered a tray heavily laden with thousands of calories. "Just put it in the center and bring a couple of empty plates, we're gonna share."

****

Jordan finished one glass of water and requested a second as she plated small amounts of each of their delicacies. They ate in uneasy silence. *At least he came out of prison with all his body parts. I wonder if I am going to hear his stomach churning as he misinterprets my silence?*

Jordan finished the second coconut shrimp and stared at the remaining food on the table and her plate. She put down her fork. Kirk stopped midchew and scrutinized their surroundings. The afternoon's live music began, invigorating the crowd with pop tunes. They sat in a bubble of silence for a beat.

"Is your food okay?" Kirk pointed at her plate and frowned.

Jordan stared down at her plate, not meeting his gaze. "It's not the food."

"Is it me? I mean, what I told you?"

She looked up at him in surprise. "No!" She hesitated. "You were so honest. I don't want to be presumptuous, but I feel I should be honest, too."

"Well, I am confused, but if it's bad enough to keep you from eating on your cheat night, you better clue me in."

She knew he expected a laugh, but she didn't have it in her. "Seven years ago, I told you I needed four months to visit family in Baltimore."

"It was a long four months. We were in the weeds without you."

Jordan's heart lifted; he'd never said that before. "The reason I went to Baltimore was because that's where Johns Hopkins Medical Center is."

"Was one of your family sick?"

"No. I was sick."

"What? Sick with what?"

Jordan finished her mai-tai in one long swallow. Kirk's eyes grew huge.

"I had breast cancer. Something my mother and sister died of." She watched his face pale considerably.

"My God, Jordan, are you okay? Has it come back?"

"No, thankfully, it worked out as the doctors hoped it would if I had … radical surgery." She finished those ominous words and slowly looked up at him. "Do you understand what I'm saying, Kirk?"

He sat in stunned silence for a moment. "You're saying you had a radical mastectomy."

"I had the breast removed, all the surrounding lymph nodes, muscle, and tissue. It wasn't pretty for a long time." Kirk nodded silently. "I had the option for less surgical invasion, but then, I'd face chemo and radiation. That's what killed my mom and sister. So I dove in headfirst and had them just cut it out of me."

Kirk covered her hand with his and sought her gaze. "I'm sorry, why didn't you tell me? I would have been there for you."

"It wasn't your job. It was your job to give me the time off. Don't think I didn't appreciate the weekly postcards." She smiled softly.

"Yeah, but if I'd known…"

She held up a hand to forestall him. "Kirk, I'm telling you this because I didn't seek reconstruction. And here's where the presumptuous part comes in. There are a lot of men who are just turned off by the imperfection. After I healed, I went to the North Shore and had an ornate tattoo inked across the incision to deal with the disfigurement. This is who I am." Jordan threw up her hands and shrugged.

She felt Kirk's gaze sweep across her torso, almost felt him measuring the sides, looking for imbalance. "You've seen me in the gym; I wear a prosthesis."

He pointed two fingers at her. "But you've never worn tank tops now that I remember."

"Right, even with my buddy, my underarm isn't right. So I wear sleeves. Of course, I'm getting to the age where every woman wears sleeves." She dug her fork into the food on her plate and resumed eating. As she chewed, she watched Kirk from under her eyelashes. She could see his wheels spinning.

"You're okay now? You keep up your checkups?"

"I've been cancer-free for seven years. That's behind me. I'm only mentioning this because I don't want to scare you."

Kirk moved his food around and reached for a shrimp. "Do you see me treating the war vets in our survivor's class differently?" He bit and chewed.

She shook her head, and her smile grew wide. "Are you sleeping with any of them?"

"No… but that's not because they have battle scars. Your battle was with a deadly enemy, too. Scars are just tattoos with survival stories."

****

The palm trees were black silhouettes against a canvas of pink and orange sky. The colors melted into the waves kissing the beach. Kirk and Jordan waved off the taxi at the front of the bar's resort and headed back to Kalakaua Avenue to watch the vanishing sun as they strolled toward McCully Street.

They held hands like kids, Kirk conscious of her soft skin as his thumb stroked her hand. "I didn't expect to hijack your day this way." He searched for her expression, peering directly into the setting sun. Her smile dazzled him. It was hard to think while walking with her, knowing what they planned last night. There was something to be said for spontaneity. Yet, spontaneity didn't cover the bases of clean underwear and a close shave. *This has to mean I'm too old for this when I have to align everything with a shower and shave.* They passed resort shops with everything from tee-shirts to diamond rings.

"Tell me about your condo…"

Jordan stopped short and made a humorously baffled face. "It's a two, two with a dining room, living room, and wraparound lanai. Are we listing it?" She playfully punched his arm. "I get one parking space. Visitors have to arrive early to claim a spot."

"Good thing I've got a bike." Kirk stalled in front of a store. "I've got to make a pit stop."

"You know, I am past childbearing age…" Her tone was dead serious.

He flustered red as he took the steps two at a time. Before he entered the shop, he turned and shot two fingers at her. "Wait, right here."

Chapter 16

Jordan fiddled with her phone and set the condo lights to a flattering level. She adjusted the ceiling fans to a slow sweep and then set 'mood' music very low. As she positioned her home for their encounter, she watched his shenanigans in the store. She looked at her reflection in the window glass and frowned. Her hair was windblown from dinner on the deck. When she rubbed one calf against the other, she was glad she kept the waxing appointment Monday.

Through the glass storefront, she watched the comedy of Kirk dodging from rack to rack, throwing items over one arm. The longer he was out of sight in the back of the store, the more nervous she grew. He burst out the doors like a kid off a school bus.

Seeing the bag sway with considerable weight, her brow arched. "What is your evil plan?"

He laughed, but his opaque bag gave no clue to the contents. The rustic linen bag was stuffed and topped off with tropical tissue paper exploding from the handles. "I got something for you, I got something for me, and I got something for us. But you can't see any of it till we get upstairs." He wore an irresistibly, devastating grin.

****

The same guard as last night sat watching multiple security monitors as Jordan used her key fob to access the lanai entrance. "Good evening, Troy, did I get any packages today?"

"You sure did, Ms. Perry. I have to say, I knew you worked at Silver SEAL Fitness, but I never expected to meet the silver SEAL himself." Kirk drew his head back in surprise. "It's a real honor to meet you, Mr. Roman. I'm in the police academy, and you and your gym are a legend to my classmates."

Jordan grinned up at Kirk.

Kirk smirked. "Glad the buzz is good." He held out his hand to shake Troy's hand. "I don't think I've seen you there. You know students get a low, low rate, especially police academy students. Drop-in when you aren't doing everything else."

"I'll do that, sir. Thank you very much."

Kirk felt the bulky police academy student's appreciation as the kid checked a clipboard and handed the Amazon package to Jordan. "Have a good evening, Ms. Perry, you too, Mr. Roman."

Kirk entered the elevator and pressed against the back wall. "I'm surprised he recognized me. Last night was the first time I've been here in how many years?"

Jordan chuckled as she pushed her floor number. "It's Troy's job to remember people and be friendly." She held her package to the side and spun to face him. They collided, and she whispered. "Worried about your reputation?"

The beginnings of a smile tipped the corners of his mouth. "My concern is for yours, madam." He held his arm out when the door opened, and she preceded him. He caught her package in his other arm as they walked the long hallway to the end of the building. *Deadman walking.*

Jordan threw open the door. "Let's get relaxed…" She kicked off her shoes, and from the collection at the doorway, Kirk saw he should follow suit.

****

Is this the same apartment I came unglued in last night? There was furniture he never noticed. How had he not tripped over it, escaping to the lanai?

Up-lights hidden among dense palms illuminated the corners, and the frond's shadows deepened the aqua walls to hues of teal. The fawn plush carpet was soft as sand to his feet. The room glowed with a rippling surreal light from the oval aquarium coffee table.

He dropped his shopping bag on the floor and knelt alongside the aquatic 'condo'. "Did I say anything about this thing last night?" Kirk read Jordan's amusement at his reaction.

"I think you flew right over it last night."

"I've never seen anything like that." He looked around the room. "You don't have a cat, do you?"

"On the twenty-ninth floor? Nope. Just my fishy friends in my saltwater aquarium. They don't talk back, and they don't drink my wine." She sat on her sofa opposite Kirk and sliced open her package. With an approving smile, she shook out new athletic wear. "I adore purple; now I have something new for work tomorrow."

Kirk sat cross-legged and chuckled. "You're thinking of work already?"

"Yeah, I've got to figure out how I can convince my boss to give me an extra hour in the morning."

Kirk crawled over to lean on her knee, still dragging his shopping bag. His voice was low, seductive. "I believe the boss may be late tomorrow." Then his excitement reemerged. "But check this stuff out." He dumped the riot of colored tissue in his lap and began sorting in two stacks. "Sorry, Nemo, you can't watch this." Kirk unfolded a modest white linen gown, displaying ornately embroidered cutwork along the provocative split up one side and laid it on the coffee table. Jordan let out a gasp as he gently spread a matching kimono over it. Kirk unfolded the linen drawstring trousers and camp shirt.

Leaning over the bounty of alluring clothing, Jordan rested her chin on her hand, a delighted smile on her lips. "Kirk, that gown is… exquisite. Exquisitely thoughtful that you chose something with more on top." He watched her hand skim it's softness tentatively, and he grew more satisfied with his choice. "Those trousers look… accessible with those pockets and the drawstring."

"Yeah, they didn't have anything for men that announces come and get me the way that gown does." Before he stuffed the tissue back in the bag with the tags and the receipt, he dropped a fabric convenience kit in his lap and condoms followed, six of them. "Besides, before I use every item in this," the TSA sized bottles rattled as he shook the kit, "you probably don't want to undress me. That's why I asked about your bathrooms. You think we might give each other a little bit of clean up time?" He ran his hand over his prickly jaw.

Leaning toward him on her elbows, her gaze softened, half-lidded as she sighed lightly. "If I haven't been falling in love with you these past eighteen years, you just iced the cake." She stood and clapped her palms on her thighs. "Let me give you the twenty-five-cent tour. This unit was set up with two master suites, and I enjoy the one with the massive tub…" Jordan held out her hand to Kirk, almost pulling him to the other end of the condo. "Both bedrooms open onto the lanai, so make yourself comfortable and meet me out there, okay?"

Kirk contained his excitement, yet his subtle smile was as intimate as a kiss. He followed her past a king-sized bed overlaid with a dramatic island quilt appliqued with deep green Monstera leaves. Floor to ceiling diamond-shaped bookcases artistically displaying hundreds of books opposite a framed museum store print of Paul Gauguin's Tahitian Landscape. No wonder Jordan was such a force of nature; she lived, cocooned in peace.

"The shower has crazy settings, play with them until you find what you like." The ample stall with the pebbled floor and teak bench invited him to forget any performance pressures. Another small aquarium in the bathroom's back wall cast an azure light, a softer choice than the brilliant LED lights over the mirror. Jordan returned from the linen closet with two overly fluffy towels, a washcloth, and a hand towel. "Call me if you need anything." He waited to see if she'd entertain an invitation to join him. "Okay?"

Jordan escaped the bathroom, leaving through the bedroom's door to the hall.

****

The privileged who live in a state-of-the-art mansion strip down, step into the shower, turn it on and presto, hot water. Apparently, folks on the twenty-ninth floor of a midcentury condo do not live this way. This mere mortal had grown accustomed to saving water by jumping in and dialing full pressure.

The tile temple echoed his plaintive cries as needle-sharp cold water horizontally assaulted his torso. Kirk spun, and his hand flew to the controls of the ten marauding showerheads that sequentially pulsed daggers. *Must get closer to end this onslaught.* With frantic blinking, Kirk saw the digital interface to this torture apparatus. Once he adjusted the temperature and water pressure, he soaped up and made friends with the plumbing.

The rain shower should have been relaxing before bed, but Kirk's mind wandered elsewhere. He looked down at himself, flag flying high. *Hey, old buddy, don't peak too soon. This evening is a banquet, not fast food. Am I jacking up a good friendship and an excellent employee? Or am I risking my heart?*

Brushing his teeth while he angled his back and hips into the horizontal spray, he grinned at himself in the shaving mirror. As he took the last stroke with his razor, he admitted he hoped she liked the way he looked tonight. He hung up his towel and stowed his duffle bag of insecurities. Giving himself a distant spray of the stuff in the kit, he hoped he wasn't too old for the cologne the kids were using these days.

****

Jordan bent over and blow-dried the hair at the nape of her neck. *Nothing more repulsive than reaching for your lover's neck and claiming a thatch of wet hair. How long has it been?* How many men did she moon over and then silently pump her fist at passing them by? Women talked. They were scandalous in their Monday morning play by plays.

For eighteen years, she picked at salads while she joined the gathering of ladies at the literary club. They were more a drinking club with a book problem. She winced at the descriptions of men's horizontal performances documented by the bedroom goddesses. At first, she wasn't over losing her husband; she was too young to be a widow. Then there was the Big C. *Stop it!*

I've seen Kirk nearly naked; I caught a whiff of his competitive sweat in a self-defense clutch. Cobalt blue eyes, hard flesh over muscles worked for a lifetime. His forearms drove her crazy with their rippling strength under a dusting of greying hair.

When the visiting ju-jitsu instructor flipped him, she remembered his horizonal belly button with the wisp of, *what did they call it, a 'treasure trail'?* Disappearing into his waistband.

Feeling confident and naked under her handkerchief linen gown, she ran her hand over her irregular right side. Cupping her full left breast, she sighed. *Babe, I hope you're enough for him.*

Jordan remembered the silly sex toy party she went to a couple of years ago. She pushed things aside in the hall closet and found the tall glass cylinder candle. Blowing the dust off the silver cap, she smirked. *I've got more dust on me than this candle.* She lit the blood orange massage candle and carefully walked toward the lanai. She listened for sounds of bare feet on tile and then heard the pop of the sparkling rosé she'd put in a chiller.

Jordan stopped short at the sight of Kirk Roman on her patio, barefoot, linen trousers hinting at his commando physique. His shirt fluttered in the evening breeze; dusty grey hair spread over a well-developed set of pecs. His hair, slightly damp danced over his forehead as he leaned over to pick up the two flutes

Chapter 17

Kirk held fast at the sight of his goddess carrying a lit hurricane candle. The flicker complimented her even, classic features, elevating her to a deity. *And she's giving herself to me?* He looked toward Heaven. *Please don't let me screw this up.* As she set the candle down on the table, Kirk teased her by moving to the lanai railing. "Come over here, and let's enjoy this view together." He held out the flute in an invitation.

She accepted the sparkling rosé, and before they touched rims, she looked at him from under her lashes. "What are we drinking to?"

"To eighteen years." Their rims clicked, and before he drank, he said, "You're the longest relationship I've ever had."

She sipped, and her cheeks bloomed. "And I don't remember any arguments. What a record." He savored the sight of her bare feet, shuffling closer to him. Her mixed scents of linen and jasmine mesmerized him as she pressed a hip to his. Her gentle hand caught his elbow as if seeking permission to come closer. He forgot about the sparkling rosé when all he wanted was Jordan in his arms, her taste on his lips.

He took her flute from her. "Let's intoxicate each other a different way." Poised facing each other, his arm slipped around her waist, and they were a breath apart, lips tasting close. His thumb glanced over her rich full mouth, and he watched his reflection in her bright grey eyes. Just as they sought a kiss, there was an explosion.

Their eyes squinted closed; the noise was enough to make two adults jump with a squeal. They fell apart, and Kirk looked at the fireworks over Waikiki Beach. "It's not Friday night…"

Jordan's hand flew to her heart with the sweet sound of her chuckle. "There's an Asian resort over there. When important people arrive; they set off fireworks for their first evening."

Kirk hooked a thumb at the show in progress. "Let's pretend it's for us." His hands sought hers long enough to kiss the backs of each of them. Then he wrapped her hands behind his back under his shirt. "This is my invitation." He kissed her forehead. "Please, Jordan, once we get this close," he couldn't press closely enough to her, "never let me go…" Kirk's lips glanced along her dancing silver hairs moving like dragonflies on the night breeze. His finger drew up her chin, and their gazes brought not so secret smiles to their lips.

Kirk drew in and savored every delicious aspect of her before they dared leap into horizontal oblivion. Her parted generously curved lips dizzied him for a split second. *What a honied bounty she truly is.* He stood drunk on her tender allure. *What am I doing, nibbling like I have to make this last…?* With the start of her next kiss at his jaw, when her hands rushed for the sensation of his back's bare skin, he struck his claim.

Throwing all caution off the lanai, Kirk caught Jordan up like a bride and focused on the expanse of bright silvery sheets in her bedroom. Plopping her in the center of the turned-down bed, he made the rounds of turning off every light.

****

"Kirk?" Jordan squeaked, watching his silhouette move with more grace than a man should. The candle on the lanai flickered with the indulgent scent of tropical citrus as he returned to her bedside.

"I sort of dropped you in the middle… which side of the bed do you prefer?" Kirk's devilishly handsome grin glowed in the candle flame.

"We're on the subject of sleeping… this soon?" Jordan rolled to her side and propped her head in her hand. Her free hand swept the right side of the bed. "Eventually, that's my pillow." She savored his figure in the dark, his tan, flat belly giving way to linen trousers skimming muscled hips. She was acutely conscious of his athletic physique and what she hoped he brought to her bed. *Is he as hungry as I am? How could he be?*

With a nod, Kirk placed the candle on the nightstand on her side. She blinked, and with nonchalant elegance, his open shirt slid down his muscled arms. As he sat on the bed and turned to stretch out before her, he winked. "I didn't need that shirt, did I? It felt like you were tattooing me with your fingernails out there."

"Did I leave marks?" Her smoky brow arched.

He tapped over his heart. "Right here, where they count."

Just breathe. Jordan arched into his claiming embrace. She fell into his arms and returned every kiss his lips initiated. Unconsciously, her hands wrapped around his neck, drawing him where he needed to be, where she wanted him. After all, he did say, 'never let me go'.

His knee nudged at hers, parting her long legs, her bronzed skin emerging from the high slit of the ivory gown. Balanced on muscled forearms, he felt weightless over her. She drew him closer, welcoming his athletic body.

His lips sought her tanned décolletage, and she fought the reflex to stiffen as his chin dipped lower. He looked up at her through long eyelashes, *the kind women never have*, and drew in a deep breath. "You know you feel incredibly edible. I could nibble on every square inch of you." With a dip of his hips, she felt his interest, and her long-held deep-freeze began a quick thaw.

All she could respond with was a soft giggle as she caught his bottom lip between her teeth. He groaned and moved to kiss along her hairline, and once he was at her ear, he drew in a slow breath. "About those pedicures." The tip of his tongue glanced along her ear lobe. "You said they were better than sex… That kit I bought has nail clippers." His lips caught the same earlobe, and her breath hitched. "Do you need a foot rub and a toenail trim tonight?" He leaned on one elbow while he fingered a tendril of her hair splayed on the pillow.

Foot rub? He can't be serious. What kind of a man brings six condoms to give a woman a foot rub? Without a verbal response, Jordan thrust her right arm around him and rolled him back on top of her. "Foot rub? Look, Roman." She leveled her best serious look directly into his smoldering dark eyes. "You didn't suffer the slings and arrows of that predatory shower to rub my feet."

His tongue danced over the cleft of her chin. "You heard that?"

"Just like you're going to hear me when you do what I think you're going to do." He raised on his palms, and gravity introduced her to the full weight of his erection. "I believe you're constricted down there…" Jordan's hands slid between the gap of his waistband and his flat belly. When her reach rewarded her with a grasp of his lively flesh, she felt his hearty chuckle rumble out of him. "Please, feel free to take those off."

"I thought you'd never ask." Kirk slid back, kneeling between her thighs, and moved to the bottom of the bed. *There he goes with that athletic elegance.* Standing with his back to her, the candlelight rippled over his lats and traps flexing as he positioned to step out of his slacks. *Good God.* His thumbs slid into his waistband as he bent at the waist and revealed the parts of Kirk she had secretly fantasized about in his videos. He wasn't jacked like the gym rats that avoided his classes and banged out supersets upstairs. His glutes would make a grown woman cry.

She knew how they felt through the linen. *Okay, no control.* Jordan made it to the end of the bed before Kirk stood up. Her palms claimed his obliques, running light hands from front around the sides over his upper thighs to stroke his glutes. "I have absolutely no restraint, Kirk." With a crush, she knelt with her body's length against his back. Her hungry lips kissed his shoulder, and with a deep sigh, she pressed her cheek at his spine. "I can't believe you're in my bed."

With another deep chuckle, he turned on his heel and caught her up to him. Eye to eye, he rubbed his nose back and forth with hers. "Technically, I'm at the end of the bed, but if we quit the chitchat, I can amaze you with my other oral skills."

He reached for the hem of her gown with a quizzical expression. She shook her head and fell back to her pillow, only pulling the hem of her gown further up her thighs. "Let me have this fantasy for just a few more minutes."

He followed her to the bed, finding that warm place between her thighs. "Fantasy?" His weight a whisper away from her made her flush, and she felt her belly quiver when his cock glanced over her sheltered mound.

"That you're not going to be turned off." Her hand covered her chest.

"Jordie, everything about you turns me on. But you're going to have to find that out as I show you…" Without pressuring her to undress, he kissed her gently across her collarbone. He whispered into her ear. "Tell me what you like." His fingers stroked the delta of her thighs. "And you know, don't feel like the floor will open and swallow you whole."

"No one is super smooth when it comes to talking about these things…" Jordan arched her back, wanting to feel closer to him. Her thumb caressed his bottom lip, and she felt the urge to comb into his full head of hair with her fingers to keep him right there. "What I can say is I would die to have your mouth on me." She glanced down between them, and he followed her hint.

Jordan came alive as Kirk sat back on his heels and began long strokes up her legs beginning at the ankle. "No foot rub?" His chuckle was evil.

"No!" She arched her hips towards him and gave a little wiggle. "But that is a wonderful beginning, come closer."

"While I'm busy down here," he stroked at the hollow of her thighs, where her flesh turned from tan to deep rose, "run your hands through my hair to lead me in the right direction, okay?"

Breathing became a priority as she watched the candlelight dance over him. *He's in the pose I've seen a million times on the gym mat.* He was kneeling, sitting back on his heels, his fists resting on his hips. *Only tonight, he's naked and he's gorgeous.* His muscle corded thighs led to a magnificent thatch of dark hair, and the root of her fantasies, his erect flesh. Her gaze followed his dark hair as it traveled up his belly to spread across his chest. His hand left one hip and she noticed him shaking his head at her. Then, he waved a long finger.

"My eyes are up here, Jordie, so are my lips."

Playfully she smacked both hands over her eyes. "I'm indulging another one of my fantasies. I've enjoyed you in athletic wear far too long."

Without a verbal response, Kirk wiped the back of his hand over his broad smile and slid to the edge of her gown. Jordan lifted the hem as his index finger lifted the lace. His lips curled bewitchingly as he eased within a breath of her. His hands splayed and caught her thighs, dragging her to the end of the bed. Jordan grabbed for the sheets evading her grip and caught him by the shoulders.

Her gown was around her waist; her trimmed bush right under his nose. Practiced lips gifted angelic kisses along her inner thigh. His hand spread over her lower belly as he found a home in her garden of pleasure.

Was it the candlelight flickering or her reality wavering as his tongue and lips played?

****

Jordie, have you ever experienced a love so perfect, your heart is completely full? A physical act so in tune your body is about to explode before we even lay skin to skin? Beneath me, with your eyes glistening with anticipation, I pray every aspect of your hope is satisfied tenfold. Every past carnal act was only gymnastics.

Kirk sensed her pleasure passing through her as easily as the blood in her veins. Almost unnoticed, she moved her legs over his shoulders, and he held on to her for dear life and love. He fixed his concentration on her involvement, how she moved into his lips, and her flesh quivered beneath his tongue. They were so in tune, so locked in the starlight inside their eyes.

When Kirk felt the slurry of her climax, warm and wet against his lips, her hips lifted in that invitation for more. Did he want to steel himself for that slow, deliberate slide within her? No, he wanted her to welcome him to the rest of her body. He wanted her to know he accepted everything she was.

Kneeling on the floor in the dark, his breathing half the speed of hers as she descended from her climax, he tugged her closer to the end of the bed. Wrapped in the joy of making her come, he sat beside her and effortlessly drew her into his lap, her legs around his waist.

They were face to face for a sliver of a second, and she collapsed against him, her head on his shoulder. "Are you okay? I didn't hurt you, did I?" His hands caught her glorious sex-flushed face, and they mirrored soft smiles. Her half-lidded gray eyes smiled at him, and the sensations still roiling within her caused her to bite her bottom lip.

"Okay? Am I okay? I don't even know the words… Did anything intelligible come out of my mouth?" She chuckled, and he felt it ripple through him. When her head was on his shoulder, he reveled in the feeling of her hair dancing on his flesh, he closed his eyes, imagining being even closer to her.

She sighed. "What was that thing you did with your hand? It felt so good to have your fingers inside me while your mouth was on me." She drew in a deep breath, and he felt the linen gown rub between them.

"You liked that?" He stroked her back through her gown, aching for the feel of her flesh against his.

"It was like you read my mind, touching me the way you did… you own me there, Kirk."

Chapter 18

The hovering scent of the expired blood orange candle, a strong tropical citrus fragrance, awakened Jordan. In near dawn's darkness, she stirred when she realized the long warm form in the bed wasn't a pillow.

Sometime around midnight, Kirk stopped his onslaught long enough to catch her eager face in his hands. "I want to see you… I want to keep these fireworks going…"

She held on fiercely, too afraid to show him the tattoo of the Red Dragon Japanese Maple limb that spread across a severe mastectomy scar or the Tiffany styled dragonfly over her heart. She held him close, the linen gown caught around her waist, but she also held him off.

Before they fell asleep, she recalled telling him, "I cannot take you into my body until I can reveal the rest of it."

His expression was pure confusion. She'd accepted his fingers and lips and tongue; she'd even offered to take him into her mouth to satisfy him. But he shook his head vehemently. "If you cannot let me accept all of you, how can you tease me with part of you?" As the moon rose over Waikiki, they fell asleep in each other's arms.

She wouldn't debate him. He was right. Why would they have this night, but build this wall between them? She slid silently from the bed and moved in the moonlight to finger comb her hair. Staring at the mirror, she raised the gown over her shoulders and tossed it to the chair. Daringly, she slid back under the coverlet and sought the heat of his resting form. With his back to her, she moved to spoon him, her hand falling around his waist. In his sleep, he caught her hand and drew it to his lips.

"A change of heart?" His voice was husky and dry.

"Yes." Jordan rolled to her back, realizing she hadn't slept on her side of the bed, and if he saw anything of her, it would be her silhouette against the indigo night sky.

She felt his hungry gaze eat up the sight of her freckled flesh. Rolled on his left side, his semi-erect flesh teased at her hip. He tucked his right hand behind his back as if he'd ask permission to touch her.

"You know you're gorgeous." It was a matter of fact, a profoundly established element by the tone of his husky voice. "May I touch you?" His hand rose from behind him, hovering over her belly.

"Is that where you want to touch?" She swallowed hard.

"No, I want to kiss right here." He pointed to her one awakening nipple.

"And then?" Another deep breath held.

"And then I want to kiss the dragonfly and every blossom on that vine."

Her breath released a split second before she caught his grizzled morning jaw in her hands and drew him to her lips. As her kiss released, she breathed the words into him. "Please, Kirk, please, do that."

****

If he felt any hesitancy to take Jordan, her words dispelled that myth. Her command both stirred and filled him with the highest intention to blow her mind with his devotion.

Seeking her pale grey eyes, he blessed her with a whisper of a kiss on her chin. "There is a fountain of youth." Kirk rested his cheek on her full breast and cherished the steady beating of her heart as it quickened. "It's in our minds. It's our creativity." Lightly, his fingertips glanced over the Tiffany dragonfly tattoo as if his fingers did a watercolor artist's work. Her back bowed into his touch and his breath caught at her response. "We'll show each other how we tap the sources of our inspiration."

Kirk nuzzled her breastbone as his tongue darted over the leaves of her scar's tattoo. As Kirk moved over her, to claim her, his hands caressed the rise and fall of her waist and hips. When he looked longingly at her from between her legs, he nuzzled her again softly, finding her cachet fragrantly sweet.

Kirk rose to his knees and then sat back, legs out. He pulled her to nestle her bush over his waking flesh. When her arms encircled him, he worked his fingers into her thick wild hair and they brushed noses, sharing a shy smile. "How are you doing? Am I rushing? Moving too slowly?"

Jordan giggled lightly, pressing closer to him than ever before. "When you're with the one you love, everything moves within its own time." Her legs caught his waist tightly, caressing his erection with her heat. "I surrender to you, Kirk, take me with you."

If that wasn't the mother of all consent, Kirk didn't know what was. He was inspired to obliterate all her thoughts about pedicures being better than sex. He wanted to ring every bell within her.

In the center of the bed, they played, his fingers traveling gentle circles around her breast, and his eyes feasting on the sight of Jordan's erect nipple. She reached for the back of his neck and drew his face to her. Cold fire streaked through him as he closed his mouth on that lone nipple. He suckled, exciting her with small spasms. Her words carried breathless abandon. "You have my dragonfly dancing within me, love."

He held her to him, his erect nipples catching a buzz from Jordan's flush of color warming her torso. As Kirk left her dark rosy nipple, his lips and tongue danced along the maple branch.

Her breathing deepened, and he stopped at once. "Are you too sensitive there?" Their gazes met, and she was speechless, only shaking her head 'No' as she caught his head to bring him over the rambling branch of ink tattooed across her. "Please, please don't stop…"

His tongue flitted and dove in gentle sensations as she rocked hard on him, her legs tightening around his hips. *How far can I extend this energy building within us?* His flesh accepted her heat, and he stiffened under her weight.

"I want this time to last forever, Jordie." Kirk whispered. He regretted releasing her legs from around him. He wanted to take her in a mound of pillows in that bed till dawn. "But, since we're going to do this, I need…" He nodded toward the accordion of condoms on the nightstand.

Jordan caught his hand. "When you were with *her*, did you use condoms?" His body froze at the meaning of the 'her'. For a second, he felt deeply guilty at his past admissions with Jordan.

"I did. And I made a trip to my doctor after the last time." He didn't know what to prepare himself for in that minuscule silence between them.

"And you're clean?"

"Totally."

"Then, I want to feel all of you. I want you to feel what you do to me."

Her words sent his heart into flight, upwards and outwards. Jordan lay before him, their energies building and crackling when they connected. Kirk relished the sensation of her hand, cupping the back of his head, welcoming him within her. Her fingers meandered through his hair, her nails penciling designs on his scalp.

Jordan released his head and trailed her fingers down his back and around his side to his navel. He gasped slightly as she stroked below his waist.

****

His breath against her became shallow and fast as she slid her fingertips down his treasure trail and cupped his hip with her palm.

His lips released her breast and he rolled onto his back. She ran gentle fingertips over the texture of his sac. She nosed his belly button and kissed his stomach. *I want to devour him.*

Jordan eagerly lowered her face to his erection and planted small kisses all along it. She expressed a wicked giggle while tonguing each side of his sac, and then circling his shaft with her tongue and lips. Their foreplay was delightfully reciprocal. Everything she did made him shudder and moan.

He reached out and stroked her cheeks and ears with both hands. Flushed and breathing quickly, she fancied she could see his heartbeat in the pulse of his thick erection.

When she felt that he could stand the teasing no longer, she slid him into her mouth and kissed hard, playing roughly with her tongue.

Kirk rose swiftly and rolled her under him. "Jordie, I'm the luckiest man on this earth." He eagerly gazed into her loving eyes as he notched himself at her waiting warmth.

With a playful tilt of her hips, she coated him, and they dove into the thrust and parry of delightful sensations. He gasped as she moved her mouth on his, their kisses muffling the sounds of their exhilaration. One of his hands stroked her hair away from her florid face, and she drew his fingers into her mouth.

His thrusts became fevered as she suckled each finger and raised her legs around his waist. With each long stroke she fought to meet his aim. *Not too much, though.* She hesitated, wanting to extend the power of this joining.

She felt his breath catch as his hips made an especially deep dive into her, her grip held him there, her ankles entwined high behind his back.

"Just for a second, don't move, Jordie." His eyes closed tightly, his face the image of elegant masculinity. In that still moment, their bodies vibrated as bowstrings plucked in a crescendo.

With a flippant thrust from below, she drove him harder, knowing he was powerless to stop her. He gasped and hilt deep, her grip on him sent them to heaven.

Kirk fell to her side, rolling her with him, refusing to leave her. Jordan rocked, continuing the ripple as Kirk cried out in surrender. "Good God, woman. Nothing prepared me for you."

Jordan rolled over him, her breast against his chest, and sought his mouth. They kissed fiercely, hungrily. She tasted herself on his lips and it excited them both. Kirk stroked her back and squeezed her buttocks. He held her tightly, and they rolled in wicked playfulness.

When their pleasuring wrung the last bit of energy from their limbs, they lay, opened mouthed and breathless. Kirk sighed deeply and held her silently, wrapped in the chaotic, mussed up bedcovers. They lay, light-headed, and sweaty. Their glow descending from their inferno.

Her voice was soft, tentative. "Do you need to leave?"

"Are you chucking me out?" Kirk asked, looking for the clock's glow in the dark.

"No, I just wondered if you had to go home before work?" She was prepared to hold him in the bed if she had to.

"Well, let's see," Kirk ran a hand through his hair, "which would I prefer to do? Ride a motorcycle home alone, or stay in bed with you? In thirty or so minutes maybe, we could have some wakeup loving?" Kirk caressed her eager face. "Tough call, Jordie."

"If you put it like that, I guess you don't have much choice."

"I'm not capable of 'putting it' any other way at all. Don't throw me out before the morning, and I'll keep your perfect body right up against mine."

Jordan grinned and snuggled up to him. "I'll enjoy your perfect body, too."

At dawn, Kirk was true to his word. They began their loving instinctually before either was fully awake. Jordan riding him. Kirk riding her, moving gently.

Kirk rose first to shower. Jordan donned her kimono and watched him like a voyeur, enjoying the sight of him lathering his pecs and scrubbing away the scent of her sex in his pubic hair. All the while, knowing she could claim him and ride him, marking him all over again.

The comforting news was that their love wasn't new. Their active loving escalated from a longer held, previously platonic level. Fortunately, both recognized their desire to give and receive real pleasure in love.

As Jordan thought about the days to come, Kirk entered from the bathroom, towel wrapped around his hips. He stood at the end of the bed, looking at her. "You okay, Jordie? I wasn't too rough?"

"I feel... renewed. Everything is right with the world."

Kirk paced the bedroom, retrieving his linen trousers, and cast away camp shirt. "So, what do we do next?"

"Next?" Jordan ran a wide-tooth comb through her hair, still not belting her kimono. "Breakfast and then we face the world." She tapped her comb on the center of his chest. "Try not to look like we banged each other all night."

She felt his enthusiasm wane through the change of his expression, but he was there in a heartbeat, his arms around her. "Jordie, this wasn't an all-night 'bang' as you called it. It was enlightenment… going off like a bomb inside me."

She felt a thrill pass from her heart to her shoulders and arms. "I didn't mean it like…" She covered her face in her hands. "I meant, how are we going to keep this a secret? Your rules about dating employees -- I am horrible at secrets."

As his hands gently comforted her, he grinned hugely and bent down to kiss her on the mouth.

"I can't keep secrets either, but you know that. So, let's not keep it a secret. I love you, Jordan. Will you be normal with me?"

Jordan's hands caught his trouser waistband, and she tied the drawstring. "Well, how can I refuse an offer like that?"

"When you put it that way, it's not as romantic as last night." He wrapped his arms around her neck and kissed her hard on the mouth. "I hope this won't be a one and done thing."

Jordan looked slightly shocked. "Why would you think that?"

"Well," he shrugged back to gaze into her eyes, "I'm not the most romantic man. I'm a little abrupt…"

Jordan put a finger on his lips and turned serious. "I want to be normal with you." She hugged him tightly and rested her cheek against his chest. His heart thumped wildly. "If last night was 'normal', I want a lifetime of normal."

Their kiss began softly, slowly but grew more profound as they strove for the closeness their hearts demanded.

Finally, he pulled away, and his crooked smirk was adorable. "You mean that?"

"Completely," she sighed.

CHAPTER 19

Wearing only her kimono, Jordan scrambled eggs while Kirk, freshly showered strolled into the kitchen in his linen trousers. He thumbed through his phone, finding several missed calls from an unknown number. He put his phone on the breakfast table and came up behind Jordan.

Strong arms wrapped around her waist as he buried his nose in her hair. "Ms. Perry, you smell like sex."

She leaned back into him, feeling him stir within his linen confines. "The best perfume there is Eau de Kirk."

He barked out a laugh and rubbed his freshly shaven face on her neck. "I thought I told you I'd take you out for breakfast."

"But if you did that, I couldn't do this…" She turned off the burner, covered the scrambled eggs, and spun to embrace him, skin to skin.

"They do frown on that in restaurants." Their nuzzling and kissing was interrupted by Kirk's phone. They glared at it and crab-walked to stay in their embrace allowing him to pick it up.

He flipped on the speaker. "Roman."

"Kirk Roman?" The mechanical voice inquired. Kirk made a face and hung up.

The phone rang again. "Roman."

"Mr. Roman, do not hang up."

"At this hour, whatta yah want?"

"We have your lover…"

Kirk's brow rose, "You do?" Jordan grimaced and returned to the stove.

"Your home and your business have been wired for surveillance. Do not contact the authorities. If you contact the authorities, we will know, and bombs will be detonated."

Kirk paced the kitchen. "Why are you shaking me down?"

"Unless the amount of forty million dollars is wired to an offshore account by midnight tonight, all of your properties will burn. You will be framed for the murder of LaDonna Garza-Mendoza. You will be contacted with the bank routing numbers."

"What do you mean framed for murder? What have you done to her? Before I pay one dime, I need proof of life."

"Check your phone." The call disconnected.

Jordan poured two coffees and brought them to the table.

"Drink this before you check your phone."

"Jordan, you know she's not my lover." He swallowed a long drink of coffee. "You know she carries on; I just don't know who she's tied up with or why they think I have forty million dollars."

His head fell in his hands. He queued the video and watched a ten-second loop of LaDonna, bruised and battered, tied to a chair with today's newspaper pinned to her filthy blouse. "Who would do this to her?"

Jordan handed him her home phone. "If they think she's your lover, they don't know about me. Use this, call the cops."

Kirk accepted the handset and stared at it for a second. He looked up Mark's number. His night manager lived in the building above the gym.

"Mark? Did I catch you before you opened the gym?"

"Yeah, Kirk, you know me, it's 6:50, and I'm right outside."

"Don't open the door."

"What?"

"Don't. Open. The. Door. Put a sign up, 'Closed for an Emergency'. And, Mark, go somewhere else today. Don't go back to your apartment."

Mark guffawed. "What the hell?"

"I'll call as soon as I can say more."

****

Des Franklin rounded the corner and nearly bumped into Mark, coming down the steps. "I was going in for a morning workout."

Mark put out a halting hand. "Kirk just called; we're closed today. Something stupid. I've got to go make a sign for the door."

Des's head tilted. "It's closed because of something stupid?"

Mark waved him off. "Look, Kirk told me to leave the building. He doesn't even want me to return to my apartment. I have no clue, but he's on it. Why don't you do what I'm going to do and head for the beach?"

"Do you have Kirk's cell number?"

Mark frowned. "I can't give you that."

Des shook his head and laid a hand on Mark's shoulder. "I have information he needs. I swear, I won't get you in trouble."

At Des's touch, Mark's shoulders relaxed, and his expression lightened. "Okay, but don't tell him where you got this." Des nodded and dropped his duffle on the sidewalk. First, he paced the depth of the building along the side street, and then the busier front of the structure.

The coffee shop across the street was the perfect place to 'think' about this one. Des bought a hibiscus tea and perched on a barstool facing the gym. The fragrant steam roiled up from the cup as he closed his eyes and inhaled deeply.

I don't see danger, but I do feel deception. A vision showed him a bald eagle, a graceful hunter, never seen in Hawaii. The large bird circled above the building and came to rest on a branch in the tree outside the gym. *It's time to look inward with a careful eye. The couple in Vegas, the warning to them, the man's relation to Kirk. This is all connected, but nothing is happening here.*

Des dialed Kirk's number and hoped for the best. "Mr. Roman?"

"Roman here. Who's this?"

"Mr. Roman, this is Desmond Franklin. I gave you tickets to my show…"

"Sorry, kid, wrong time for a review."

"No, sir, it's not that. Please, hear me out." There was a beat of silence.

"Do you know what's going on here?"

"You mean at your gym?"

"The gym, my house…"

"Only your gym, sir. You've been told there's danger. But you've been deceived. I get the sense nothing is happening at your gym."

"Of course not, it's locked tight…"

"No, that's not my meaning. There is no danger in your gym.

"Look, kid…

"Sir, weeks ago, I met your son."

"Are you in on this extortion con?"

"No, sir."

"Don't interrupt me, young man…"

"Sir, weeks ago, I gave your son a warning. His wife is in terrible danger. This is all about money, lots of it."

"Listen, Des…" Kirk pinched the bridge of his nose. "Why don't you meet me at my house? I'll text the address, okay?"

****

On Jordan's house phone, Kirk called Jax.

"Who are you and why are you calling at this hour?" Jax roared into the phone as he rolled off Kameo.

"It's your father. You don't recognize this number because I'm afraid they've tapped my cell."

156

"What have you done?" Jax drew his hand across his mouth as Kameo scowled and rolled over, pulling up the sheets.

"It's what you've done. Meet me at my house under the porte-cochere in fifteen minutes. Do not approach the door. We have a situation."

"Where are you now? What number is this?" Jax rose from the bed and hunted in drawers for undershorts and clothing.

"Son! This is a pipe hitter situation. Get your wife and your ass to my house."

Jax slid into clothes and yelled for Kameo.

****

Jax and Kameo hunkered down in the Jeep under the porte-cochere when a bronze Toyota hatchback pulled in behind them. Jax jumped out of his Jeep, gun drawn. "Step out of the car, put your hands on the roof, spread your legs." He motioned with the gun barrel.

Desmond threw up his hands. "I… come in peace? I told Kirk I'd meet him … he's expecting me. Guess I beat him here?"

Jax advanced toward him carefully and studied the man's face. "Xavier, the Oracle?"

"I'm Des to my friends." The man shrugged with a warm smile, still in arrest position.

Kirk and Jordan arrived in her diamond white E-Class cabriolet, the blue top discreetly up.

Jax holstered his gun and shook his head. "What the hell is going on?"

Kirk gestured to Jordan. "Jordan Perry, meet my son and his wife. Jason and Casey Rawlings."

Des pointed a finger from Jax to Kirk. "Son, Father." He pumped his fist. "I knew it."

Jordan shook her head. "What are you doing here, Des?"

He threw them all a bewildered look. "What am I doing here?"

Kirk shook a finger in Des's face. "Jax, you know this man?"

Jordan and Des exchanged a confused look.

Jax circled Des, his thumbs caught in his belt loops. "Yeah, he flipped us out for days. We tried like the devil to figure out what he meant. The guy's got a hell of a handshake. Did you shake his hand?"

Kirk slid his hands in his back pockets. "No, why would I? I've been to his mentalist show; he's a member at the gym."

Jax nailed Kirk with a look. "What's going on, Dad?"

"I got a call early this morning telling me a woman from the gym was kidnapped. I am to wire forty million dollars to an offshore account, or she will be killed, and I'll be framed. They said if I called the police, they'd know, and the gym and my house were wired to explode." He gestured to Des. "Then this kid calls and says there's no danger at the gym and I am being deceived. I have a suspicion he's in on it."

"Me?" Des squeaked.

Jax fumed. "So, you had us meet at a place wired with bombs?"

"According to your psychic, there are no bombs."

Jax impatiently reached out a hand for Kirk's phone. "You have proof of life?"

Kirk nodded and scrolled to the video. Jax's lips drew a straight line as the image appeared. His cheeks colored, and the flush traveled down his neck. He forwarded the message to his phone and returned Kirk's cell. Jax dialed Gideon. "I'm sending you a video. Your target is active. How far out are you?"

There was a beat while Gideon played the video, and he returned. "I'm at Flint's. I'm twenty minutes out."

"You son of a bitch, you've been here all this time? I'm at my dad's. I'll send the address; it's around the corner from my house."

He heard Gideon gathering his weapon and heading for the car.

"Yeah, I didn't want you to be nervous now that you're retired and all. We've kept eyes on you. I like Kameo's brown bikini better than the green one."

"I'm telling her you said that." Jax closed the call and texted the address. He turned a piercing gaze on Kameo. "No more bikinis."

"This day cannot get any stranger." Kameo commiserated as she watched Kirk stare down Des about the threats. Jordan stood back from the family, closemouthed.

Jax strolled back to the group. "You can let him off the hook, Dad. He has nothing to do with this."

"How are you so sure?" Kirk scowled, pushing his sleeves up, ready for a fight.

"The gym member you called LaDonna is the jefa of a Mexican drug cartel. My DEA team thought she was dead, until the new team alerted Gideon, that she's alive."

Jordan clapped once loudly. "I knew she wasn't a nice person."

Jax nodded. "We liberated thirty-nine million of her dollars to assist a family the cartel terrorized over decades."

"Thirty-nine million is a good start."

Jax stepped back at Kirk's flippant remark. He gestured to the mansion. "Where'd you get your good start? Was this part of the inmate rehab program?" Des and the women backed away warily. "Are you sure she doesn't think you're mobbed up? That's why she's asking you for forty million?"

The two men, one the junior image of his father, squared off. Their backs were ramrod straight, feet shoulder-width apart and knees flexed, ready to pounce. They rested their fists on their belts, identical cobalt blue gazes threatening hellfire.

****

Kirk's voice, low pitched and steely, admonished his son. "I'm disappointed in you, Jaxson. I've never done a thing to deserve this scorn. This house is not mine. I'm the property caretaker. I generally live in the casita in back."

Jax's eyes grew wide with surprise. "Then why did you invite us to 'your house' and entertain us on the patio? By the pool, you talked about the outdoor lifestyle…"

Kirk dropped his head and nodded. "Evan Silver spends about a month a year here. He gives me free run of the place. I regret misleading you."

"What about the gym, you turn a nice profit…"

"It's Silver Seal because Evan Silver owns fifty-five percent of it. It has taken me fifteen years to earn my equity."

Jax scrubbed at the back of his neck and drew in several deep breaths. "You got anything else you need to tell me?"

"No, no, nothing else to tell you." He looked down and back up at his son. "Now this thirty-nine million, Jax; Kameo said she'd come into a little money before you moved here. It wouldn't happen to be thirty-nine million, would it?"

Jax shot an accusing finger at Kirk. "You don't know what they did to her father, in front of the family. Kameo was a child; it was savage." There was silence among them all.

"But that's the money she came into?" Kirk persisted.

Jax nodded at Kameo, who nodded along with Jax.

Des dug in his backpack as the family conversation grew more embarrassing. "Anybody have some gum?" Kameo fished through her purse and offered him a pack. His fingertips touched hers, and the two of them fell apart. He stared at her. "This isn't over. There are no bombs, but the target is not the woman in the video. Their target is Kameo."

Chapter 20

A black over black Hellcat screeched tires as it turned into the driveway and swerved to avoid the people. Gideon and Flint emerged from the sportscar. "You park in the driveway; you don't stand there, too." His gestures were as large as his voice was loud.

Jax smacked him on the back of the head. "You've been here all this time? All you know is my wife's bikini colors?"

Kameo and Jordan echoed, "What?"

Kirk ran a harried hand through his hair. "Who are these men?"

Gideon walked up, followed by Flint, and offered their hands. "U.S. Marshal Gideon Sullivan, Professor Flint Tomas, former CBI. You must be the tree," he gestured to Jax, "this nut fell from."

Jax crossed his arms over his chest. "We've solved your case for you. How nutty is that?"

****

Within Kirk's casita, Desmond sat with Jordan and Kameo while the four men circled the breakfast table.

Gideon got off his cell and jotted down an address. "I've got a safe house on Round Top Drive until we catch LaDonna; that's where Kameo and Jordan are going." Gideon stared down Jax's nonverbal objection. "I've got an unmarked car coming for them within the hour." He turned to the women. "These places usually have a common stock of toiletries and simple clothes; you know a few muumuus. You'll be comfortable and safe."

Kameo paced in front of the window facing the ocean. "Comfortable? Safe? It's all coming back to me now. A windswept cliff, a waiting helicopter. The promise that we'd be safe." Her voice escalated with tension as she spoke each word.

Jax shrugged to Gideon before he approached his wife. "Baby, you know you're still the target. What am I supposed to do, use you as bait?"

When she turned from the window, tears rolled down her cheeks. "I'd feel safer trailing you than being separated from you." Jax caught her in an embrace, kissing the top of her head and whispered.

Gideon interrupted the moment. "Let the professionals handle this." When he turned back to Flint, he caught the sight of Kirk watching Jordan's posture harden. "You got a problem?" He gestured from Kirk to Jordan.

Kirk's gaze shot angry fire. "I'm finally with the woman I love, and we're going to put them in the hands of strangers and go into battle?"

"These deputies are trustworthy; I know them from San Diego. I'd trust them with my son." Gideon watched as the formidable Kirk wrapped Jordan in his arms and pressed kisses on her forehead and ear. "You *are* going into battle. Do it knowing your loved ones are safe."

Jordan lifted her gaze to the men and back to Kirk. "I know he's right. I don't want you worrying about me when you need to be battle focused." She glanced at Kameo. "Casey and I will be waiting for all of this to be done." Jordan pinched Kirk's cheek. "Besides, I'm not done with you. Hell, we haven't even begun…"

****

Flint Tomas stood at the door of the Papu Circle home. Three knocks, nothing. Kirk and Jax circled the home as if it were booby-trapped. Nothing but the clamor of a game show from the back of the house.

Kirk approached the front porch, angered. "I've stood right here and heard her cursing at someone in Spanish. Probably the person with the blasted tv."

162

Jax took his position to breach the door, Gideon's hand fell on his shoulder. "You got your credentials?"

"No…"

"Then, you and Pops need to step back. You're retired."

Jax scowled and joined Kirk and Flint off the porch.

"On the count of three." Gideon nodded. The door flew open, no deadbolt. The television grew louder as they approached the family room.

"Federal Officers."

The young girl threw up her hands. "Show me your hands. Don't book me." Her parroting of American television was flawless and frightened.

Flint spoke to her in rapid Spanish, and she slowly lowered her hands.

She peered at them from under dark lashes. "La patrona?"

"Si, LaDonna Garza-Mendoza?" Flint gestured around the home and produced an old photo of Isabel. "¿La conoces?"

The teen nodded vigorously. "Si, Isabel Huerta, la patrona."

Gideon pushed forward and pointed at her but spoke to Flint. "This one here knows Huerta? Who's she?"

As rapidly as Flint could translate, they determined she was Consuela, a teen from a Mexican convent school. The girl answered every question promptly. Around every third response, she asked haltingly in English, "May I have asylum?"

Kirk returned from one end of the house with a birdcage. "The only papers I find are dead presidents." He peeled up layers of newspaper to reveal cash. In rusty Spanish, he asked, "Is she holding you here against your will?"

Consuela's eyes went round and grew wet. "Si."

Jax returned from LaDonna's bedroom with a selection of semiautomatic weapons. "These were next to her Louboutins."

Gideon approached Jax. "This is LaDonna's house girl, so far she hasn't revealed any knowledge of what's going on other than LaDonna left around ten-thirty this morning."

Flint went to the garage and called Gideon. "Look at the wall, doesn't that look like the video? There's the chair and the newspaper."

In the two-car garage, one bay held a late model black BMW. "She's not driving her car. We can't Lojack her, can we ping her cell phone?"

Jax called out from the kitchen. "The cell is off, can't ping her."

Kirk paced the house, frustrated. "Until she makes the next move, we're dead in the water."

Jax bellowed, "Gid, I need you a moment." Gideon finished a sentence over his shoulder and slid the kitchen door closed. "If you're really with the task force, where's your team?"

The blonde US Marshal stalled his growing grin and turned away to look out the kitchen window. "I've got Flint and two SEALS. What more do I need?"

"Dammit, Gid. Is our ass hanging out for target practice?"

Gid made a time-out gesture. "The local Marshals office did supply me with an unmarked car and the use of their safe house."

Jax scowled. "Did you tell them why? Can we trust them?"

Gid pinched the bridge of his nose. "I told them I needed a safe house. I didn't mention Huerta. Enough of this trust crap. They're the Marshals Service."

"They didn't ask who needs to be safe?" Jax moved into Gid's personal space, hands on hips.

"I said I had a possible suspect under surveillance. I needed a short-term hiding place."

Jax leaned flat palms on the breakfast table. "We know LaDonna is Huerta. We know she targeted Kirk to get to me about the money. We know Des was right, you had the places swept.

There were no bombs or surveillance equipment in either location."

****

Kameo twisted her length of hair this way and that, indecisive of how to tie it back while Jordan shoved boxed food back and forth in the kitchen pantry. "I'm sure eventually this is going to be nerve-wracking, but right now, I'm bored to tears."

Jordan nodded. "Not very stimulating, but my view is, while it's nice to have all these big strong men protecting us, I'm glad I know some self-defense to protect myself."

"I never had the chance to study martial arts, would it even work in real life?"

Jordan pulled down microwave popcorn and prepared a pack. "Martial arts improves your self-confidence and situational awareness, but for women our size, a bigger guy is going to win in a street fight if he catches us." Jordan found paper towels and bowls while the corn popped in the microwave. "Our strategy is to escape. I can show you a couple of moves." Kameo decided to tie her hair up with a clip. "Great idea, hair is always an easy grab. The next thing you want to do is… come at me and grab my right wrist with your right hand."

Kameo thought the process through and attacked. She was met with a fierce downward slash of Jordan's left hand. Jordan spun away and was in the next room in seconds. Kameo gawked. "It's that easy?"

"In real life, maybe not, but while you're fighting this person off scream bloody murder, the average attacker gets scared, too." After sharing popcorn, the two women took turns, attacking and repelling each other in different ways.

Kameo fanned herself and returned to the family room sofa. "I guess I worked off that buttered popcorn. So, how long have you known Kirk?"

165

****

Kirk opened the garage door while Jax searched the BMW's front seat. "Dad, did she mention looking for a new place to live?" Jax rose from the car with a plastic bag full of real-estate flyers. He dropped them in a laundry basket and dug back between the seats, looking for any other revelations.

Kirk searched the glove box, and Jax looked up at his "Aha." Jax repeated, "Aha?"

Kirk held up the SVI Tiki with an ink pen through the trigger guard. "This baby is a museum-worthy work of art that also happens to fire bullets, only a cool four grand."

Jax shook his head. "Four grand? When you could carry two Ed Brown Special Forces guns for what she paid for that piece of jewelry?"

"If she left this one here, can you imagine what she's carrying?"

The men moved to dig in the back seat, and when their gazes met, Jax confessed, "I don't want to think of what she's carrying right now." The men declared the backseat cleared, and Jax carried the basket back into the house. "Maybe the convent girl will recognize one of these properties."

Sitting at the large dinner table, the men spread the flyers to hold up like flashcards for Consuela.

Flint held up a colorful brochure for a service called Steamy Yoni. He glanced at the name. "What's a yoni?" Consuela giggled and looked from man to man. "Some new food craze?" Gideon took the brochure from him and spread out the accordion pamphlet.

"Not the way you're thinking." Gideon turned his back on Consuela and mouthed the words. "They blow steam up their twat."

Flint's dark skin flushed red. "That can't be right. Let me see that." All the while, the teenager's shoulders shook in suppressed laughter. "Good God, that is what they do."

Gideon never blinked, with a flourishing gesture, he proposed, "Now, you know what to get Mavis for your anniversary; she has everything else."

Flint flipped the flyer back to him. "Pass."

Jax fanned a collection of high-end condo brochures and held them up. "This looks like a serious real estate hunt to me..."

"Senor Tomas, 'Ike Nui…" Consuela grabbed at the stack and slid them away until she found the flyer. In rapid Spanish, she recounted how many times her patrona drove by and made her sit in the hot car while LaDonna spoke with men in construction hats.

Kirk's phone trilled. "Roman."

The mechanical voice spoke. "Do you have a pen and paper. Mr. Roman?"

Kirk drew himself up to his full height as he paced LaDonna's dining room. His voice was light, almost jovial. His smile came across in his words. "I don't think I need a pen and paper." There was a play of static and indistinguishable words. "I had some friends check out my house and the gym. There are no bombs, never were."

"Mr. Roman, pay the ransom."

"Or you'll kill her and frame me? I've done prison time, and now, I have far better witnesses. I'm not playing your game."

"You don't care if the woman dies?" The distorted voice grew outraged.

"No skin off my nose. I thought about it. I don't think she's worth forty million. Hell, not even forty k."

"You have sealed your fate. Everyone shall die for their sins." The call clicked off.

Gideon pounded the table. "Couldn't get a trace on the call; we lost it somewhere in Tunisia."

Jax arched a brow. "It ought to motivate her to do something."

****

LaDonna unhooked her burner phone from the voice distorter and dialed.

"US Marshals Office." The professional voice answered.

"Deputy Divine, please." LaDonna requested and heard the click of the transfer.

"Deputy Divine."

"This is a concerned citizen." She could hear him snap to attention over the phone.

"Yes, Ma'am."

"I'm especially concerned about a woman I believe may be on the island under a false identity, running from criminal activity."

"Do you have a name?"

"I was just given the name. It's Casey Rawlings."

"Your call is valuable, my concerned friend. This system has recorded your number, and we will be in touch."

****

George Divine was no longer a 'runner'. He'd served enough time in the both the Marshal Service and under the payroll of the Lobos Cartel, to send underlings to do his bidding. He'd been grooming Deputy Manu for just such an opportunity. "Manu!" He called crisply. "I have a name for you to run down." He slid him a piece of paper.

Manu was more than a little surprised to find Casey Rawlings was a safe house resident. He raised a hand in parting at Deputy Divine and headed off for a personal meeting with their concerned citizen.

Chapter 21

Deputy Ben Young stirred from his uncomfortable slump on the foyer's tile floor. He looked at his watch, *last time I looked at it, I was answering the door. It was a minute past one PM.* He stumbled to his knees, then held on to the wall to get to his feet. His mouth was dry, his head swam. Cautiously, he drew his weapon, he was unsure of the nature of the threat, but he was sure there was one.

Gun barrel preceding him, his sluggish tour throughout the home delivered bad news. Both women were gone, no signs of a struggle and his partner at the back door was still waking up. He re-holstered his weapon and returned to the foyer. The view of the neighborhood from the porch was 'Wonder Years' ordinary.

Ben walked to the foyer mirror and looked for injuries. On his neck, he saw a sloppy needle mark. He slipped out his phone and prepared to give Gideon the bad news.

"Hey, Gid, remember what you said about the snitch in San Diego?"

Gideon drew a deep breath. "If you're gonna tell me, you have one too; I'll let you face two former SEALS alone."

There was a beat of silence. "I'm sorry, man. They're gone. I can't even tell you how. I was knocked out so fast. They used drugs, and I've got a spot on my neck, might be an injection site."

His partner moved sluggishly toward him. "What the hell happened?"

Gideon cursed under his breath. "How long were you out?"

Ben eyeballed his partner. "About an hour."

"Don't report this, Ben; this is between you and me."

"You know that's not protocol."

"Give me at least a two-hour lead."

****

Flint urged Consuela to put the birdcage into the back of Mavis' SUV. He made sure when he spoke to the young woman that he spoke slowly and made good eye contact. He could tell she'd been an abused hostage. He looked at his wife in the driver's seat. "She speaks mostly Spanish and television English. She's excited about leaving this house." He hooked his thumb back to the mansion. "Take her home, feed her lunch, and let her talk about the bird. She loves that bird. If she says anything about her keeper, jot it down." He kissed two fingers and placed them on Mavis' cheek. "Just reassure her that she's safe."

****

Gideon stood in the center of LaDonna's home and bellowed. "You are not going to believe this."

As Jax and Kirk entered from one side, Jax grunted, "Yeah, I think I probably will…"

Kirk folded his arms over his chest. "This can't be good."

Flint returned from the driveway. "What's going on?"

The team looked at Gideon, his blonde hair standing in sharp contrast to his red face. Both hands fisted as he described his news. "The island has a snitch. About an hour ago, someone knocked out the two deputies. The women are gone."

Kirk and Jax pulled out their phones; the father looked at his son. "Do you have any calls?"

Jax shook his head. "Nope. That frightens me even more."

Gideon paced, head down as he shared the report. "We don't know who took them. The perp used short term injections on both my men. There was no sign of struggle, so I'm assuming the women were taken at gunpoint or also drugged. The deputies are canvassing the neighborhood, but I don't expect anything."

Jax and Kirk immediately turned to their phones, dialing Kameo and Jordan. Both phones went directly to voicemail.

Kirk charged to the refrigerator and pushed aside imported Mexican sodas, dug out a six-pack of Dos Equis, and dropped them on the breakfast table. He took one can, shook it, and partially opened the top toward the wall. "Piss on LaDonna and everyone she associates with." When the can was empty, he followed the same with the remaining five beers.

Gideon pulled Jax aside. "Is this you in twenty years? Cause, I've never seen you waste alcohol."

Jax's cobalt eyes turned steely. "I haven't begun to plot what I'm going to do with LaDonna when I catch her."

Gideon nodded and then pointed to the group. "Let's sit and brainstorm our specific objective."

Jax pushed past Gideon to take a seat. "Brainstorm a specific objective? This killer has no cartel behind her, but that's never stopped her from cold-blooded murder." Once seated, they waited for Kirk. "Dad, enough, get in here. Sit down."

Kirk approached the group, steely-eyed and grim-faced. "How do we bring her down?"

Gideon turned on his tablet and considered his limited resources. "Who has access to the facial recognition software used on this island? Anyone? Cause I am not calling the Marshals office for a paperclip."

Kirk's expression brightened. "Evan Silver, my benefactor, has written some of the most accurate programs. You need someone to hack into them?" The other three men listened carefully as Kirk called the software business magnate's son. "Jerry, this is Kirk. I need your expertise, are you near your computer?"

****

The carpet cleaning van pulled up to the condo's garage gate. One delicate hand held out Jordan's key fob, and the gate rose. "Remember what I told you. Silence. I need to untie you for the walk to the apartment, but I have a gun with thirteen bullets." Jordan and Kameo nodded in what passed for silent understanding.

Jordan took the lead, with LaDonna walking closely enough to hide the gun stuck into Jordan's back. Each time they approached a surveillance camera Jordan mouthed *Help me.*

LaDonna whispered in Jordan's ear. "If you have a security system, disarm it. You don't have one of those pesky voice control things, do you?"

Jordan shivered as she fumbled the key in the door. She looked over her shoulder. "I usually unlock my door with my phone, but you have my phone."

LaDonna sneered at her and patted her jacket pocket. "You no longer need any means of communication."

Jordan considered slipping out of her shoes, then reconsidered the opportunity to land a better kick with her deck shoes.

Ladonna burst past Jordan, to confirm they were alone. Manu hurriedly moved to drop all the blinds or draperies at each window. Ladonna barked her difference of opinion. "We're on the twenty-ninth floor. No one knows we're here. Leave the windows alone and bring two dining room chairs into the living room. Tie their ankles to the legs and their wrists to the sides."

The eager to please deputy tossed all the closets for rope or duct tape and finally brought a king-sized sheet and used his knife for ripping strips of the cloth.

Jordan barked, "That's Egyptian cotton…" The man balled up a small piece, shoved it in her mouth, and secured it with the first strip.

"Shut up. I hate women who talk too much."

Ladonna prowled the room with the gun pointed in their direction. "I can smell Kirk here." Jordan shook her head no. LaDonna tapped the gun barrel on Jordan's forehead. "I said I can smell Kirk here." Jordan dropped her gaze to the floor. "I can smell him on you." LaDonna backhanded Jordan.

Jordan closed her eyes, recounting her last conversations with anyone who meant anything to her. *Why did I let my embarrassment over my body get in the way of pursuing Kirk? We could have had years together, and all we had was hours.*

While Jordan's eyes were closed, she felt the angry motion of the deputy tying her wrists and ankles. She heard Kameo squeak with the force of Manu's knot when he bent over to secure her ankles. Then after a sacred moment of silence and darkness, Jordan considered opening her eyes to see if they'd been blindfolded. The suppressed sound of a gun went off within feet of her ears. Kameo screamed.

Jordan's head swiveled to see Kameo's golden complexion blanche to white. Manu lay on the floor, a pool of blood blossoming from the exit wound in his face.

"Witnesses are messy, Ms. Jordan. When I am done with Kameo Alana, both of you will be at peace."

LaDonna opened a phone. "Dr. Alana, what is your father's phone number? He's in Michigan under the name Charles Adams, am I right?" Kameo closed her eyes tightly. "You seem surprised that I know." Kameo nodded blankly.

"I've known about your assumed names for weeks. What I didn't know was that Roman was stupid enough to marry you. Then he changed his name. You people are crazy for your subterfuge. That's what private detectives are for."

The ripped strip of fabric in Jordan's mouth inevitably migrated to the back of her tongue. What started as a tickle became a cough, gagging and finally choking. Jordan's nostrils flared with air hunger. She saw stars and was grateful when LaDonna turned her attention to her. Long, sharp nails scratched her cheek as LaDonna ripped the gag from her mouth. She gasped for air, coughing with tears streaming down her cheeks.

LaDonna bent her knees and got in Jordan's face. "Every time I approach my goals, there you are! You're the speedbump in my life. I set my cap for Kirk, and you run interference. I seek this one," LaDonna waved her gun at Kameo, "and there you are. What is the game? Whack a mole?" Jordan violently shook her head, still coughing. "What does he see in you? You have no style; you have no elan. Why does he want a little grey mouse?"

Jordan shut her eyes, desperately attempting to look like the mouse LaDonna raved over. Tied up and helpless, she was in no position to challenge a crazy woman with a gun, but self-defense taught her to bide her time and watch for cracks in her opponent's assault. *This will be my life or hers.*

"…how much do you think you'd be worth to him? Bastard said I wasn't worth forty thousand? What's your worth?" LaDonna's fury escalated.

Jordan glanced at Kameo who's eyes warned her to stay silent. Kameo's voice was low pitched and deliberate. "My father doesn't answer unfamiliar phone numbers…"

LaDonna turned on Kameo. "Oh, another subject heard from. You're as ready to get this done as I am." She shook Kameo's phone at her. "I'll use your phone. Call him at the clinic, tell him it's a medical emergency." LaDonna pressed the clinic number.

Chapter 22

Jax led the men to his pool house, nervously jingling a large ring of keys. Kirk mirrored his son's anxiety. The men stood in the doorway of Jax's 'pool house of freedom'.

Gideon crossed the threshold and gaped at the four diamond plated walls hung with guns. "I see what you did here, and it's a pool house outside, the windows are fake. Unlock the door, and this is where you'll hold off Armageddon."

Flint approached the wall of sniper rifles and leaned into one in particular. "Hello, old friend. Jax, what are you doing with *my* Henry 'Long Ranger' Rifle?"

As Kirk signed in on his tablet, Gideon took inventory of the guns present. "How did you get these on the island? I don't want to know."

Jax threw up his hands. "Every one of these is in my real name. This is all perfectly legal." Clockwise they ranged from the smaller handguns all the way to an Armour Black Chey Tec M200 Intervention, an exceptional sniper rifle accurate to twenty-five hundred yards. "Some men collect fishing flies; I collect guns."

Gideon pointed to the arsenal. "You knew this day was coming."

Jax grimaced and tilted his head noncommittally. "I like to be ready for anything. Flint, now you are too. You left to be a professor and left your rifle behind. I knew the rifle was valuable." Flint retrieved his sniper rifle and sat at the cleaning table, taking it apart and checking each piece. Jax tossed him the ring of keys. "Red key gets you into the ammo safe." Jax pointed to a door.

****

LaDonna put Kameo's phone on speaker and issued terse directions while the clinic's phone menu played. "Everything in your bank accounts needs to be wired to a number I will provide. If you tell him you are being threatened, I will make your death slow and painful." LaDonna waved a fancy handled straight razor under Kameo's nose.

"Chris?"

"Casey? This is Melody. Your uncle had to accompany a critical patient off the island. He's in a copter headed to the upper peninsula. I expect he'll check in after his patient is admitted. It should be a couple of hours." Kameo's eyes watered, and she blinked until fat tears traveled down her cheeks.

"Would you tell him I love him?"

"Well, sure, honey. Is everything okay? You haven't had newlywed buyer's remorse, have you? You know that hunk of a man, Brody Glenn was sniffing around…"

LaDonna covered the receiver. "Shut her up."

Kameo tried laughing. "Oh, Melody. I just miss Uncle Chris. I'll wait for his call. Bye, now."

LaDonna tossed the phone on the sofa. "A smart girl like you must know your bank account number."

Kameo shook her head, and her tears flew. "I don't know my father's bank account number. Even my account requires my signature and my husband's for any transaction of over ten thousand dollars."

"Well, isn't that regressive thinking? You have to have your hubby's permission to spend your money?" Ladonna bent nose to nose with Kameo and ran the razor lightly down her forearm, drawing a pencil-thin line of blood. "This blade is so sharp you barely felt that, didn't you?"

Kameo's gaze widened in horror at the slowly pooling blood. *I didn't feel it. Shock. I'm in shock.*

LaDonna ran the back of the blade across her cheek and loosened the messy bun on Kameo's head. "Well, it seems we have a couple of hours… to kill." Kameo and Jordan's gaze flew to the dead man on the carpet. "I can tell you a couple of things about that husband of yours." LaDonna's chuckle was lusty and sinister.

LaDonna keyed Jax's name into her phone's Google search and held up the image search results. "Do you see one Asian girl in any of these photos?" LaDonna scrolled through dozens of images of Jax with voluptuous blondes. "It seems he has a type. I'm surprised he hasn't asked you to bleach your hair." The tension in the room caused Jordan and Kameo to break out in a full sweat, even though every window and sliding door welcomed the island's trade winds.

Her captor caught a hank of Kameo's mahogany hair and pulled it out tight. LaDonna hacked at hunks of hair, leaving an inch or two in various patches. "Jaxson Roman is a playboy. My men were amazed at the women he fought off even while he worked. Did he make you sign a prenup that required you keep your shape?"

Kameo set her jaw in an effort to curb her sharp rebuttal. She knew anything could earn her a slashed throat. She counted the carpet loops. More and more of her dark hair covered the floor as LaDonna's verbal barbs were paired with the blade's attack. Then there was silence. There was no more hair on her shoulders to cut. *What will she cut next?*

LaDonna reached into the tote bag and withdrew a long dark wig and a jar. Making a show of it, LaDonna covered her red hair with the dark wig. She opened the jar and waved the pasty red hair dye in Kameo's face. "Better red than dead." With both hands, LaDonna massaged the dye into Kameo's shorn hair. The dye's waxy texture spiked Kameo's hair in every direction. When LaDonna was satisfied, she bent over; dyed hands held out. "Don't you make a cute redhead?"

****

Kirk wiped at nervous sweat on his forehead. "Evan's son got me into the local facial recognition programs. A man drove a van with LaDonna in the passenger seat. They were last seen at a traffic light at McCully and Ala Wai about thirty minutes ago." Gideon and Jax exchanged flummoxed expressions. Kirk chimed in, "That's within walking distance of Jordan's condo." Kirk's phone vibrated in his back pocket. "Roman."

"Mr. Roman, this is Troy at Kapiolani Arms…"

"Troy, I'm putting you on speaker." Kirk turned up the volume. "Go ahead, son, what is it?"

"I believe Ms. Perry is in danger. She lip spoke *help* to all of our cameras between the garage and her unit. There were three people with her. An Asian woman," Jax balled his fists and cursed under his breath, "a man in a suit and a woman who looked like she was hiding a gun in Ms. Perry's back."

"Have you told anyone else?" Kirk asked.

"Ms. Perry hasn't set off any of the silent alarms. She's probably been threatened."

"Troy, I'm here with a US Marshal and members of the DEA. Don't notify anyone. Don't acknowledge this is happening. We're on our way."

"Come to the employee entrance; I'll let you in."

Flint spoke up. "What's the closest building with a parallel floor? I need access for surveillance."

Troy hesitated. "Vista View is next door; their rooftop access will get you almost even with her unit. I can call their security desk."

****

In tears, Kameo croaked out, "If I can get the hacker who stole your money to put it back, would you leave us alone?"

Those words snapped LaDonna out of her preening with the wig in the mirror. "I would have to think about that…" She bent closer to Jordan. "Too bad you got mixed up in all this. You just don't know how to pick 'em."

Jordan whispered. "Well, maybe not, but if you kill us, do you think Kirk or Jax will ever leave you alone to enjoy your millions?"

LaDonna scrunched up her nose. "Hmm. Hard to say."

"I think there are dozens of beautiful places in the world where forty million dollars would last several lifetimes. But if you kill his bride, you can run from Jax Roman, but you'll only die tired and broke."

LaDonna stood up abruptly and retrieved Kameo's phone. "I'm sure your hacker is in this directory, right?" Kameo nodded slowly. "Who's number?"

"Norah, just Norah."

LaDonna dialed the number and set the phone on speaker. "You can keep the interest; I want my thirty-nine million."

The phone rang and went to voicemail. "Norah, this is Kameo, I really need you to call me. You have my number. Please, it's urgent."

LaDonna snapped the phone shut and backhanded Kameo across the face. "Voicemail? Is this a trick?" She snatched up the razor, turned, and menaced Jordan. "You may be right about Jax hunting me down. Are as sure about Kirk?" She shot a sly look at Kameo. "Are you willing to watch me kill your friend slowly? You're a doctor. How long does it take to bleed out?"

"No, it's not a trick; they're six hours ahead of us. Try Jonah's number…"

LaDonna fumed. "Seriously?" The phone rang, caller ID said 'Norah'. "Don't play games." LaDonna took the call on speaker and held it out to Kameo.

"Norah?"

"It sounded serious, honey. What do you need?" Norah never called her honey. It was not a term of endearment in this Army veteran's vocabulary. LaDonna held out a business card with a string of numbers.

"Norah, I need thirty-nine million deposited to an account in Belize. I have the routing number."

"Honey, it's going to take a hot minute, you've got several accounts. Let me get started, can you text me the numbers?" LaDonna nodded and began texting the info.

"Please, rush it, Norah. I need to come clean. We were wrong to take that money." As Kameo spoke, a grin grew across LaDonna's face. "Can we stay on the line with you so we can get the confirmation?"

Cheerfully LaDonna nodded as she dug a tablet out of her purse and logged into her waiting bank account.

Norah's voice came through. "Honey, I'm going to put the phone down while I move this money with both hands."

Wide-eyed, LaDonna watched as deposits began arriving.

Chapter 23

Jax's phone rang as the men sped toward Jordan's condo. "Jax," Jonah's hearty greeting boomed through the phone, "tell me your wife hasn't had a change of heart?" The former intelligence operative spoke cautiously.

Jax barked back, "What are you talking about?"

"Flash, are *you* secure? Norah's on the line with Kameo right now."

"Music Man, I've got the team heading over for an extraction. Huerta has Kameo." Jax rubbed at his jaw.

"Flash, we figured something was up." Jonah chuckled. "You know, you don't have thirty-nine million to move? Not to worry, what we're doing is a boomerang hoax. Huerta will see the money, get a confirmation, and by midnight, it will evaporate. Got that? It sounds like you're moving on this, I'll let you go."

Kirk's jaw set as he approached an empty intersection and blew through the red light. "Let 'em chase me; we can use the backup."

"We can't use the sirens," Jax exploded.

"On the twenty-ninth floor in this city, it's background noise." Kirk gunned the accelerator.

Gideon held on in the front seat. "I appreciate the spirit. Right now, as soon as LaDonna gets her money, this is the women's crisis hour. We have no idea if LaDonna will cut and run or use that scorched earth mentality she's known for."

Jax leaned forward. "Get Flint and me to the Vista View employee entrance. We need eyes on her."

Kirk nodded his head back to Flint. "I like the caliber of Flint's eyes better than yours, Jax."

"That's why he's carrying the sniper rifle."

****

LaDonna grinned madly as the last deposit hit her account. "Tell your friend a nice thank you, and you have to go now."

"Thanks, Norah. I love you guys." Jordan watched sadly as tears streamed down Kameo's cheeks. LaDonna dropped the phone on the floor and stomped on it.

Of all the behaviors Jordan witnessed from this poisonous woman, she sensed new and frenetic energy. *What did the gal at the fitness center call her crazy roommate? Bugnut? LaDonna has gone five hundred percent 'Bugnut'.*

"Time to change your clothes, my sweet." LaDonna untied Kameo's wrists and dragged her dress over her head. The criminal turned to the hall mirror, once again preening to look more like her hostage. LaDonna removed her dress, kicked it aside, and donned Kameo's. She disappeared into the bedroom.

Jordan and Kameo exchanged silent amazement that LaDonna neglected to retie Kameo's hands. While LaDonna's focus was on vanity, Jordan carefully leaned back to test the looseness of the fabric binding her ankles to the chair legs. Since the man tied her, she'd been flexing and pulling to release more fabric from the knot. Jordan silently signaled to Kameo as she heeled off her deck shoes and slid one ankle free and then the other. She pushed back into her shoes and sat with her ankles close to the chair legs, waiting for her chance at LaDonna.

Jordan turned awkwardly to catch an angled view of their captor in the small mirror hung on the living room wall. She signaled to Kameo with her eyes, and they both observed LaDonna draw up two syringes. The women exchanged somber expressions and nodded in grim unison.

When LaDonna's humming grew louder, they saw her prancing toward them, a syringe in each hand. Jordan counted the steps, anticipating LaDonna's assault first, she was closest. Jordan held her breath.

LaDonna bent over the back of the chair to deliver Jordan's injection. As Jordan exhaled, she surged up, the chair back hitting under LaDonna's chin. The syringes flew from her hands as she groused indecipherably with a bloody, bitten tongue and fumbled to recover.

Kameo rocked her chair over LaDonna's body, and the two women wrestled. Jordan, hunched over with her wrists still tied to the chair, hustled to the lanai, screaming "help" all the way. LaDonna fought out from under Kameo and crawled around, seeking the syringes or her gun. Kameo hurriedly ripped her ankles from the chair legs and landed punches and kicks wherever she could. They wrestled steadily toward the lanai as Kameo struggled to get the syringe out of LaDonna's hand.

LaDonna managed to plunge the needle, but Kameo broke free before the dose was entirely delivered. With a scream, Kameo ripped away the syringe, fluid spurting in an arc and plunged the long needle into LaDonna's thigh.

Jordan worked out of her wrist bindings and began throwing patio pillows and cushions over the railing for attention. When LaDonna and Kameo grappled closer in death's dance, Jordan snatched up a pineapple sitting in the fruit bowl on the lanai table. She held it like a baseball bat. With one small step into the fray, Jordan swung her fruity weapon, and the spiny surface caught LaDonna's long-haired wig. There was a pop, and LaDonna froze.

****

Flint and Jax lay prone on the Vista View roof. Flint's sniper rifle focused on the busy lanai. His long legs spread apart, toes pointed outward, in a sniper's pose. "This is a hell of a catfight, who's who?" His trigger finger extended along the frame of the rifle.

Jax trained his binoculars on the fighting duo. "Shoot the brunette."

"What?" Flint's eyes never left his target.

Jax barked, "Do it, shoot."

Flint prayed and shot.

****

Jordan heard the crack of the shot and watched LaDonna lurch over the low lanai railing, plummeting twenty-nine floors. The condo front door bounced off the wall, and there was a rush as Gideon, Kirk, and Troy lept over the dead man in the living room. They arrived as the pineapple stuck in a wig followed LaDonna down, down, down.

Kirk ran to Jordan, soothing her with a bearhug. "What did she do to you?"

"I'm okay, but…" Jordan turned to watch Kameo collapse in Gideon's arms. "LaDonna injected her with something; there's another syringe in the living room…"

Gideon caught Kameo and laid her gently on the sofa as Troy called 9-1-1.

****

Jax pressed his earpiece closer. "What did she do to Kameo?"

"She's breathing; we got an ambulance en route. We've got the second syringe and the bottle's in LaDonna's bag. Head over."

Jax scoffed. "Like you have to tell me…"

Chapter 24

Jax knelt next to Kameo, caught her face in his hands, and tried to wake her. Kameo's eyelids fluttered at him. "I feel numb."

Jordan rushed from the hall with LaDonna's bag. "What she used is in here." She dumped the bag in front of Jax. He held up the bottle. "Lorazepam."

Kameo drew a deep breath and slurred. "Good, I'll be more awake soon." Paramedics with a stretcher arrived at the condo. "I don't need a hospital." Kameo garbled. "Just give me some Flumazenil, and I'll be fine."

The chief paramedic looked at the syringe handed to her and shook her head, comparing the volume in the syringe with the bottle's label. "If the label is correct, this is a lethal dose."

Kameo sighed sleepily. "She only got part of the dose into me. I should be fine."

The paramedic checked the cardiac readout and crouched next to Kameo. "I agree. Your vitals look good. Your Pulse-ox is fine, but we want to dress this wound on your arm. You might need stitches. Besides, how are you sure it's actually Lorazepam?"

"I appreciate…concern. Clean the wound; use steristrips… fairly sure it was Lorazepam. Not going to a hospital."

Jax shrugged. "You heard the doctor. Let's get her the antidote; the lady wants to get home. I'll watch her twenty-four-seven."

The paramedic nodded and looked up at Jordan. "How about you, ma'am? The left side of your face is bruising and swelling as we stand here."

Kirk held Jordan on his lap, soothing her wrists where she'd ripped out of the bindings. Jordan gaped at Kirk. "Is it bad?"

Kirk kissed her cheek. "You're going to have a shiner. Got any frozen peas?"

Jordan was appalled. "Kirk, you know I eat fresh vegetables."

He looked at the paramedic as the woman began Jordan's neuro check. "We'll take a couple of those ice packs."

The paramedic finished taking a blood pressure, pulled the stethoscope from her ears, and gave the okay. "She's doing fine. I assume you know how to check for concussion?"

Kirk nodded. "I've got it covered."

Jordan slid off his lap. "There's luggage in the hall closet. I've got to pack some things. I'm not staying here."

The police officer slowed her with a hand. "We're at a murder scene; we'll get your bag packed."

Kirk caringly swept an arm around Jordan, as another HPD officer approached her. "Ms. Perry, were you the individual who grappled with your assailant?"

Jordan stopped, sending a smirk to Kirk and then the young officer. "Both Kameo and I did. I was the last one."

"We need your statement…"

Kirk cut off the officer with a glare. "Ms. Perry will stop in tomorrow with her statement. Now, I'm taking her home." They got a couple of steps further, Kirk turned back to the officers and winked. "Don't ask about the pineapple in the pool."

The officer silently watched them leave.

****

Within the hour, the condo was crawling with HPD detectives. Gideon pulled the head detective into Jordan's bedroom and closed the door. "Detective Palakiko, notice how I haven't called in the US Marshals?"

186

The native Hawaiian nodded thoughtfully. "I did notice that. What's going on, Deputy Sullivan?"

"The man carried out in the body bag was from the Honolulu Marshals office. He got tagged to assist LaDonna in kidnapping the women, and then, he got snuffed. We had a problem in San Diego with cartel infiltration. You know Garza-Mendoza and Isabel Huerta, head of the Lobos Cartel, is the same person?"

The Detective looked at his notes. "Do you think there is a bigger problem than Deputy Manu?"

Gideon walked to the window and watched the coroner's cleanup below. "A deputy at his level wouldn't be a real asset to a cartel. They have to own a higher rank. I'd be looking for the next level up in the Witness Safety Division."

Detective Palakiko nodded. "I'm sending both bodies over to the coroner as a John and Jane Doe. Let's see who squirms when Manu doesn't report."

"I like the way you think. If you work with me, perhaps we can tie up the cartel's involvement in the Marshals Service." Gideon put his hands in his pockets and turned back to the detective. "That will give me a chance to check in like everything is hunky-dory." Gideon handed over a business card. "Please get officers out to this address and interview these two deputies. I trust them; they know Huerta's track record."

****

Jax walked from the front door with the food delivery bag. "Did anyone call Des? I'd like him to know how it all fell out."

Kirk walked from the guest bedroom hallway. Phone in hand. "I'll ring him up."

Jax put the bag on the kitchen island. "Tell him we've got victory food. Come get the feedbag on." Jax spread out the feast, dug into the fridge for beer, and brought them back to Kirk, Gid, and Flint. "Dad, are the ladies sleeping through dinner?"

187

Kirk looked over his shoulder at the chaises on the lanai. Both women napped under light coverlets as the sun began to set. "Looks like it."

Gideon took a long swig of beer. "We've already got Kameo with the choppy red hair. Put some big sunglasses and a hat on her, and we could sting the perp nicely."

Jax barked, "Are you crazy?" He held up his thumb and forefinger. "She was this close to death." He shook his head, his fists at his waist. "If you need a stand-in, get a policewoman."

Gideon grinned. "It was just a thought. We do have LaDonna's and Manu's phones. I'm waiting for the perp to get nervous when they can't reach Manu tomorrow."

The doorbell rang, and Jax walked Des back to join the men. Amid greetings, Jax gave him a hearty handshake. "Your vision was spot on with one tiny consideration."

Des looked around the pleasant scene of food and liquor and smiling men. "Spot on, how?"

Flint winked and nodded. "You should have seen my face when Jax told me to shoot the brunette."

Jax sat on a barstool and crossed his arms. "LaDonna wacked off Kameo's hair, thinking she could sneak out as her hostage. When they wrestled on the lanai, Flint took her out. There was a graze wound in her throat, but I think it was the twenty-nine-story fall that did her in."

Des made a face and didn't directly swallow his beer. "Jeesh. So, Kameo's okay?"

Jax pointed to his sleeping wife out on the patio. "Yup, thanks in part to you. It was a team effort. She and Jordan got their licks in, too."

Chapter 25

Kirk and Jax staggered from their bedrooms in search of the aroma of brewing coffee. Seeing Kameo at the stove, Jax rubbed the sleep from his eyes. "You never came back to bed."

"Jordan and I woke up around three and couldn't believe what we'd lived through."

Jordan leaned on the kitchen island, bleary-eyed. "I wish I could have gotten a solid hit on that bitch. But, the sight of her flying over the railing with the force of that gunshot? That was something I'll never forget." She blinked hard and refilled her teacup, and then smiled. "Kameo's making brioche French toast, live a little, skip the egg white omelet."

Kirk held Jordan from behind and nuzzled her neck. "I want to eat you up. I'm so damn grateful you're alive."

Jax poured a cup of coffee. "Dad, not in front of the kids…"

Kirk looked up and smacked the large kitchen island. "Don't tell me you haven't blessed this island." Jordan buried a giggle and slid out of his embrace to set the table.

The doorbell rang, and Flint stuck his head inside the open door. "It's me. Mavis and I come bearing Leonard's malasadas."

Kameo squealed and ran to hug Mavis; their visits had been few since Mavis still worked fulltime. "Malasadas usually aren't allowed in this house, but since we nearly died, why not? Did you get any guava?"

Mavis grinned. "The full selection, two dozen. I'm sorry I can't stay, we dropped Consuela off at the Mexican Embassy, and I have to pick her up in a couple of hours."

Kameo dragged her into the kitchen. "Just long enough for coffee and these fried fat bombs…"

Flint was already speaking softly with Jax and Kirk when the two women joined them. Kameo queried. "What's the whispering?"

From the lanai, Gideon boomed, "I'm back from my morning swim, anything to eat?"

Jax held up a warm malasada in his face. "Eat this."

Gideon garbled words as he chewed. "You got a room I can rent?"

Jordan's hip bumped Kirk. "I know a condo you can get cheap. Full disclosure, there were two murders there."

Kirk nodded. "Yeah, you'll need new carpet."

Gid chewed. "Tempting, but my son is in San Diego."

Jax gulped some coffee. "After we finish this delicious breakfast, what's the plan, Deputy?"

Gideon poured his coffee. "About that… We know someone at the Honolulu Marshals office was loyal to the Lobos Cartel, long after it disbanded. We have LaDonna's phone. I think we should text the number she called just before she hit the safe house."

Jax wiped at his lips with a napkin. "Good luck with that. As you know, I'm retired."

Gideon arched a brow as he fidgeted with a pencil. "I heard that, but it didn't stop you wanting to break down LaDonna's front door." Gideon tapped a pencil on the island. "We think a text might drag our mole into the sunshine."

Kirk swallowed a mouthful of forbidden fried dough and shrugged. "You don't think this deputy is on guard? It's been twenty hours since the last contact."

Gideon nodded. "He might let his guard down a little if he saw LaDonna driving her car with the top down."

Jax grabbed Gideon's hand. "Give you a manicure and a red wig, and you're on!"

"I appreciate your faith in my acting skills, but I don't think I'm good enough to fool him closeup." He raised a brow at Kameo. "On the other hand, a female redhead of your build would be aces."

Thumbs hooked in his belt, Jax drummed his fingers on his hips. "We had this discussion last night."

Kameo stepped between them. "Wait a minute. Let's talk about this."

Jax glared. "There's nothing to talk about."

Kameo kissed his cheek. "I would love to get a little something back from the Lobos Cartel."

Kirk reached for a malasada and smirked. "Well, you kept your thirty-nine million."

"Transactions on the internet don't count." Kameo rubbed her hands together gleefully.

Jax paced around the kitchen island, head down. "You're going against a career law enforcement officer with criminal leanings. He's armed. He's suspicious." Jax shook his head vehemently. "You missed getting shot yesterday. I'm not going to risk losing you today."

Gideon jumped in. "We set this up, texting back and forth... Propose a public meeting place... Lots of tourists, lots of cars... Flint on a rooftop. She'll be perfectly safe."

Jax slanted him a skeptical gaze, but Kameo won the argument. "I really want to do this. I'd love to bring down the last piece."

****

Kameo texted the number tagged USMS in LaDonna's phone. 'I'll leave the tote bag with your payoff near the surfboard rental shack on Queen's Beach.'

191

'What? Where? No good. You need to be there with the bag. That way, we both have something to lose.'

Without consulting the team, Kameo typed back. 'I'll be standing between the shack and Waikiki Wall.'

'What time?'

'This morning.'

'Okay. Make it 10:35; everyone else will be in staff meetings.'

'I'm a redhead.'

'I've seen your photo.'

'Since I came to the island?'

'I know who you are, Isabel or LaDonna, or whoever you're going as this week.'

****

Kameo drew in a deep breath and pulled herself up to her full height, looking up from the phone. "I'm meeting him at the Waikiki Wall at ten thirty-five."

Jax was on his feet. "Whoa, whoa. Meeting him? That was not the agreement."

Kameo shrugged. "He insisted. He says that way, we both have something to lose."

"I don't want you to have anything to lose. No way."

Gideon stepped forward. "Let's calm down, we don't have to scrap the sting. That's what back up plans are for."

Jax's face reddened. "You're crazy. She's not trained in close-quarters combat. If he gets her in a car, she's dead."

Kirk agreed. "If you think there's a backup plan, what is it? I don't see one. I agree with Jax, call in a policewoman."

"It's already nine; there's no time to pull in a cop. It would take warrants. We'd be tied up in procedure until tomorrow at 10:35."

Flint stared at the monitor's satellite view. There's no place for me to take a sniper's shot."

Kameo sipped coffee. "Why are you all assuming the worst? Maybe he wants to ensure exactly what he said."

Gideon shot her a look. "We're suspicious by nature. It keeps us alive." He snapped his fingers at Jax. "What number rule is that?" Jax shot him a middle finger salute. "Nice."

Jax shook his head. "I'm still against this. If you insist on being reckless," he shot her a frustrated look and became 'the Commander', "we'll all have earbuds. We need to look at…"

****

Deputy US Marshal Ben Young and his partner Marty Park were fully recovered from their Lorazepam dosing yesterday. Both acknowledged they owed Gideon Sullivan a favor. It was no hardship to watch the front and back of the Prince Kuhio Federal Building. After all, the reputation of their agency was in doubt. They wanted to catch the mole more than anyone. The Witness Safety staff meeting started approximately seven minutes ago. Deputy George Divine was the only officer who ducked out when he should have been there.

Gideon's phone rang. "This is Young. I've got eyes on him. The name is George Divine. Male, Caucasian, approximately six feet, two hundred pounds. Early forties, greying brown hair, dressed in a brown suit, white shirt, striped tie. Getting into a white Ford Explorer, auto tag HKN seven two eight." Gideon gave his thanks and closed the call.

At the rendezvous point, Flint blended into the shrubbery across the street at the Aloha Memorial. Using his monocular, he scrutinized every white Explorer driving down Kalakaua Avenue. "I've got him. He should meet Kameo within the minute."

Kameo stood, wearing a large white straw hat, oversized sunglasses, and an insanely patterned red and purple dress that Kirk chose from LaDonna's closet. She balanced from one foot to the other while Divine approached purposefully. Under her breath, she acknowledged. "I see him."

She let her bag drop from her shoulder to her left hand. The warning Jax gave her months ago in the prison infirmary came back like a lightning bolt. 'The best equipment in the world is no good unless you're ready. Be ready at every moment to take advantage of a situation.' She felt the Taser in her dress pocket and exhaled.

As Divine stepped into her personal space, she flinched back. *He's Hispanic, good God, I can't speak Spanish.*

"Buenos días mi amor."

In her best-accented reply, she spat back, "English."

He pulled her into a firm embrace. His hands roamed her loose dress, feeling the bulletproof vest and the Taser in her pocket. She slapped his hands away. "Oh, no trust, are you wearing your dress armor today?" Without showing it in his hand, he slid the Taser into his jacket's breast pocket. "I'm crushed, after what I did for you."

Kameo shook the beach bag against his leg. "Take your hands off me. Here is what you earned, take it, and go."

Divine let her out of his embrace long enough to pull a small handgun from his pocket and wrap one arm around her. "I've got another earning opportunity, but you must help me." He pulled her toward the running SUV.

"You have this wrong. You help me. I'm done." Each sentence of accented English caused Kameo more concern.

"Not today." He waved a manicured finger at her as he opened the passenger door and waited until she belted in. "Don't bother trying the door. I've modified the locks." When he crossed in front of the SUV, she tried. He was right.

Chapter 26

Jax was in SEAL mode now. "Goddammit, I knew it."

Gideon's voice conveyed his disappointment. "He's armed, and he's forcing her into the SUV, I'm in pursuit." He sprinted for his car.

Jax keyed his ignition. "Dad, are you in position?"

Kirk gunned his bike. "I'm on Monsarrat Avenue."

****

Traffic was sluggish at best on the one-way street. Divine cursed under his breath as he inched forward, his foot moving from gas to brake pedal to keep from rear-ending the ragged biker ahead of him.

Kameo measured her words. "Why kill the golden goose?"

In her earpiece, she heard Flint's calm voice. "The traffic snarl is in a quarter of a mile. Keep him going. We hear you clearly, good job."

"You may be the golden goose, but I've found a platinum flamingo." Divine gave a sinister chuckle. "It seems Joaquin Trevino wants proof of your death. You keep resurrecting. That's disturbing to the remaining cartels."

Kameo harrumphed wordlessly.

Divine gloated. "The Trevino family had no problem devouring your client base. They only seek a clean transition period." Kameo stretched out her long, tanned legs and played with the hem of her dress. "Playing the lady card again, Isabel?" Kameo shrunk against the passenger door with a resolute frown across her overly painted lips. "You died once; now you have to do it for good."

"Who writes his snappy patter?" Flint quipped.

Divine slammed his hand on the steering wheel as a careless driver pulled his junker of a car in front of the motorcyclist in front of him. The biker dropped his Harley to the pavement. "Ah, great, street fighting." Divine looked left and right. Cars zipped past him on the left, and vehicles parked along the right side of the street blocked his huge SUV from passing.

Kameo summoned her soft Spanish accent. "Patience, this too will pass."

Divine shot her a sideways glance. "You're calm about dying." The car's driver jumped from his beater of a car and menacingly waved a wrench at the biker. The biker swung a chain at the younger man.

Kameo silently measured the distance she would have to climb over the center console to get out of the SUV.

"Damn, cager, you cut me off," Kirk yelled, playing the irate biker who swung the chain beside him. "Look what you did to my Harley."

Divine shook his head. "That bike isn't damaged, he's just looking for a fight. Idiot."

Kameo shrugged, watching Divine's neck turn red in contrast to his tight shirt collar. Annoying chatter burped in spurts on his unit radio. The more carefully Kameo drew breath, the more agitated Divine became. He stuck his head out the window and flashed his badge. "Can you move this aside? I've got official business."

Jax grabbed his crotch. "I've got your business right here, fat man." Kirk ran up to the SUV and jumped on the bumper, menacing them with the chain. "If you're the cops, get this reckless driver off the street."

Divine ground his teeth. "Step off my car, sir."

Kirk dropped the chain on the hood and smacked it with both hands. "Why don't you get your ass out of that rolling living room and make me?"

Flint chuckled in Kameo's ear. "Don't you love street theater?"

Jax advanced, and sideways fist-punched Divine's front bumper. "Hey, dickless wonder, you gonna send the lady out to fight?"

Kirk doubled the length of the chain and jumped beside Divine's window. With the chain's snap, the window shattered.

"That's it." Divine was out the driver's door, gun drawn. "Both of you, on the ground, hands on your heads."

Jax dropped to one knee, all the while verbally taunting Divine. "Big man can't come from behind the door? Your gun do your talking for you?"

Divine slammed the door behind him and stood, gun trained on Jax. Kameo caught her gasp before it reached her lips. *Why does he do this? Taunt someone holding a gun?* Kameo gauged the coming fight and slipped over the console to sit, knees up, both feet flat against the door.

"Come and get me, fat boy." Jax laughed as he dropped to his second knee, his hands behind his head.

Kameo made eye contact with Kirk, who gave an imperceptible nod. Slowly unlatching the door handle, she was free to kick the door into Divine's back.

Divine's itchy trigger finger let off a round as the door hit him squarely with force. He teetered forward, regained his balance, and aimed the gun at Jax. Kirk tackled him from the side, wrestling for the Glock 19. Using the gun's weight, Kirk landed a powerful blow to the side of Divine's head. The deputy, stunned, slackened his grip on the weapon, and Kirk sent it sailing into the middle of the street. Jax leapt to his feet, grabbed the gun, and waited with arms crossed over his chest for his father to put Divine on the ground.

Once Kirk's knee was in the suited man's back, he felt for the cuffs on Divine's belt. "It's easier on you if you don't squirm." He locked the cuffs in place and pulled Divine to his knees. "Come on out, Kameo, I've leashed the beast." Kirk shook Divine by the suit coat collar. "Citizen's arrest."

The Honolulu Police rolled up on bicycles. "Deputy Sullivan?"

Kirk nodded down the street. "I imagine that's him running to join us."

Gideon jogged up as he retrieved his badge from his belt and turned to Divine. "George Divine, you are under arrest for kidnapping, attempted murder, and a laundry list of other brutal no-nos. Anything else we can think of, we'll work out at the station." He brought Divine along. "You have the right to remain silent… Do you have the judgment to do so?"

CHAPTER 27

After Kirk connived with the HPD officer stationed outside the condo, the officer let Jordan slip in for her the rest of her clothes. Kirk empathized as he watched her move through her broken world.

Furniture toppled and destroyed — paintings askew — lamps broken on the floor. *There was a hell of a battle in this place.* Kirk didn't need a psychology degree to know she wouldn't be comfortable living here again. And perhaps that would work out fine for what he had in mind.

Jordan moved from area to area in silent observation, like the faithful making the Stations of the Cross. He watched as her expressions revealed her pain. Her fingertips righted the gouged canvas of the koi fish. *That needs repair. How impotent must she feel at the invasion and loss of her sanctuary? I can't give her a cliffside mansion, but we have options.*

Kirk gave her privacy to roam the rooms until he heard her mournful sobs. He followed her into the bedroom, where she clutched the coverlet to her face. She hid from the slashed bedding soiled with violent blossoms of red hair dye viciously staining where they'd made love. *LaDonna took out her rage for me on this bed.*

Does she want to cry it out? Do I intrude on her mourning?

Without words, Kirk wrapped strong arms around her. Her tear streaked face rested on his shoulder, and she began to sway in his arms. He comforted her, his hand gently stroking her hair. It was a struggle to not see her vulnerability as an invitation to make everything better. But who was he to know what she needed? All he knew was that he loved her.

****

Several pieces of luggage in hand they headed out the door with the HPD guard. Jordan suddenly stopped. "I almost forgot the fish."

Kirk shook his head. "Those fish are blessed; how did everything get turned on its ear and that aquarium is untouched."

"It's immovable. But I need to go back and feed them."

"How much of a shock to the fish would it be to move your aquariums?"

She waved him off. "HPD won't be here forever." Kirk let the subject drop.

****

Kirk's front door closed, and Jordan caught him in a playful embrace. "My hero! Not only brings down the bad guys but talks the police officer at my condo into giving me the rest of my clothes."

"Well, damn, Jordie, I didn't know police negotiations would turn you on."

"Every day with you amazes me."

He moved his long, muscular body closer, crushing his hips into her. Her arms entwined his neck, and she kissed him in sensual invitation. "We're on day three, pace yourself." Kirk was immediately enthralled by the feel of their arms wrapped around each other. He kissed her slow and deep. "Why didn't we do this sooner?"

Jordan grinned. "We've been busy all day."

His finger pressed gently on her lips. "I meant, years ago." His hand ran over her hair, and he caught her face up to his. "For too many years, all I did was think of you."

200

She grinned up at him. "Well, are you thinking about me now?" She began pulling his shirt from his jeans.

"What are you thinking about?"

"While you were thinking about me, I was thinking about you. And we were thinking about each other. Too much thinking." Jordan's busy hands found his zipper. His jeans dropped to his ankles with a clunk, weighted by his wallet and keys. He'd slipped into his jeans this morning commando, thinking they were just out for a quick trip.

Jordan's eyes widened. "I thought you were bare under there. Naughty boy. What was on your mind?" Kirk grinned a satisfied male grin at her reaction.

"I want you right now," he growled, barely able to keep from tearing her clothes off.

Jordan stood, arms out. "Ravish me, Kirk, just rip these clothes right off me. 'Cause I brought the rest of them here." She let him wiggle her shirt and skirt off her body, and he tossed them forgotten to the floor. He hesitated before he unhooked her bra, and she smiled, releasing the front hook, and letting the bra join her other clothing.

Her body is a work art. The Tiffany-style dragonfly hovered over her heart, and the garden of maple blossoms waited for his attention. Kirk wanted to worship her. He dropped to his knees in front of her, kissing her abdomen as his thumbs slid into the sides of her panties, drawing them down.

Her hands moving sensuously over his shoulders. His lips moved steadily down her body, inhaling the scent of her wild arousal. Kirk nudged her legs apart with firm strong hands, draping one slender leg over his shoulder and leaned her into him. She shivered in anticipation, Kirk looked up and grinned at her, using his thumbs to move her sweet rosy petals apart.

God, she was pink, glistening, and delicious! His tongue stroked her, and she whimpered and fisted her hands into his hair. He held her hips tightly and pulled her against his face, his tongue delving into her and doing beautiful things. Jordan cried out, encouraging him. Kirk smiled and held her fast. His tongue moved to her center, kissing her deeply, and exploring as if he was kissing her mouth. Jordan's quivering body goaded him to use his thumb on her. Kirk played her like a precious instrument. She shook in response. His mouth returned to his joyful work, and he laved her lovingly. Jordan's standing leg collapsed, and he lowered her gently to the floor as he continued his sensual assault.

She arched up sharply against him. He tightened his grasp. "My sweet Jordie, you're delicious." Her arms reached around him; her muscles shook with the power of her impending orgasm. Kirk trapped her between his lips and flicked her with his tongue. With a strangled cry she came, spasming around his fingers like a velvet fist. *Oh my God, I can't wait to get inside her.* Kirk cupped the outside of her sex, rubbing soothingly as her body stopped its shaking. She lay there panting and exhausted. He rolled against her and pulled her to him.

"God, Jordie! You're enough to make a good dog break his leash!" He teased. She smiled dreamily, too depleted to do more. Kirk brushed back her hair and kissed her sweetly. "C'mon. Let's get off this floor. I want you in bed." He stood and offered a hand to pull her up.

Their eyes were inches apart, the better for Kirk to see the sweet freckles on her nose. Touching foreheads, they exchanged a breath. *This island practice is so infrequent now.* Exchanging *ha*, the breath was connected with Hawaiian culture as a sign of respect and spiritual power. *Doesn't our love bring us spiritual power? I need her beside me every day of my life.*

Her ripe lips left his mouth hungry, as they trailed across his throat to his ear lobe. She nibbled and breathed lightly into his ear. "I've dreamed of this moment, and you feel even better than I remembered." Licking her thumb and index finger, she painted across his nipple as her lips traveled to his chest. Nipping, nibbling, kissing, blowing in such a pattern and rhythm, it dizzied Kirk. "Make love to me."

He quivered on the verge of climax when her hips arched up and caught his eager flesh. Warm, inviting, luxurious, they moved together. Kirk felt Jordan shudder as she rocked gently to invite his thrusts. Her wealth of hair framed her delightful face on her pillow. *She's an angel.* They stroked together, and she pulled him close to nuzzle his neck. In his ecstasy, Kirk half expected her to nip him. Her heat swallowed him and triggered the fireworks between them.

"Come with me," Jordan implored, lifting herself with her hands around his neck and kissing him. "I want to feel all of you." He lay over her and sank himself to the hilt. Kirk lovingly regarded her face. Jordan's lips parting, ohing, her mouth open in a silent song. Jordan's smoky eyes closed and then suddenly opened, staring up at him with real vulnerability, mixed with hunger and amazement. He could feel her reaching another climax, and he almost stopped because he didn't want all this to end.

Each time he stopped, he knew their eventual orgasm would become more powerful. Each interlude would send them streaming closer together. But as he slowed his pace, she quickened hers. Her grip had a plea in its strength, an undertaste of hunger. He slipped his hands beneath her rump, so no matter what their bodies did, they would be touching, and he would stay in her as deep as possible.

They came, first Jordan and then Kirk, moments behind her, holding each other, and their cries joining, forming one wild and unbearably lovely song.

****

Jordan slid out of the shower stall after Kirk. He waited with a sumptuous bath sheet to wrap her tightly. "I need to make an honest woman of you."

He held her tight as she giggled. "I am a brazen hussy to let you go wild all over me. I'll give you a year to stop."

"Just a year?" His voice softened, and his expression grew serious.

Jordan stroked his cheek. *Oh, what did I say? Did I misspeak?* She watched Kirk turn on his heel and leave the bathroom, his towel tenuously wrapped around his slim hips. She closed her eyes and worried this would all be gone when she opened them. While her eyes were closed, Jordan sensed Kirk in front of her. When he spoke, he was down on one knee, an open ring box in his hand.

"Jordan Perry, how about we make some new rules together? Will you be my wife?"

Jordan gulped air to keep from falling over. She joined him on the floor, and they cocooned in their bath sheets as he slipped the ring on her finger. "Do we have to go out tonight?"

"If we don't join the crew, you can't show off that sparkler."

Jordan moved her hand right and left, watching the LED lights ignite the sparkle of the one carat round diamond caught by six prongs on the rose gold band. "Nice, well, maybe on second thought, I can thank you properly for this later?"

Chapter 28

Gideon paced pier eight, hands in pockets jingling his change and keys. He looked at his watch. "It's four forty-five, Jax, doesn't your dad adhere to schedules?"

Jax shrugged as he leaned on the pier railing, one hand casually caressing Kameo's hip. "I don't know; maybe he slipped back into my kitchen to christen the island." Kameo buried a giggle.

Gideon shook his head. "You're a sick man, Roman."

Flint and Mavis strolled toward them, laughing together, Flint stopped to kiss her neck. Gideon gestured with one hand, airborne. "What is it about this island, it makes everyone act like oversexed teenagers."

Kameo leaned into Jax's embrace and giggled. "Don't pout, Gideon, your plus one will be here soon. I'm sure you and Brody will have lots to talk about."

Gideon spun on his heel. "Yeah, you fix me up with an ex-boyfriend of yours?"

Kameo deadpanned. "He was never my boyfriend. He arrived on Mackinac Island to make a film, and he cut himself. I was his doctor. He gave Jax and me a very nice impromptu wedding."

Gideon groused, "I'll chat, but I won't dance…"

Kameo grinned. "He won't ask you. He usually has a girl on each arm. Hey, you can be his wingman."

Gideon glowered as the tall Scotsman strode dockside. "Good evening, friends." He caught Kameo in a quick kiss, and it was Jax's turn to glower. Jax took Brody by the shoulder to introduce Flint and Mavis as the rest of the waiting diners stepped aside to let Kirk and Jordan run to their group.

Kirk smiled a broad satisfied grin. "Sorry about that. We underestimated the time we needed to come from my place." Jax and Kirk shared a hug, and Jax smacked his dad on the back one too many times. He whispered to his father. "I think you underestimated how much time it took to come; you smell like sex."

Kirk withdrew from his son's embrace and shook his head. "Son, when I'm with her hours feel like seconds." Jordon blushed at his innuendo. Kirk held up Jordan's hand with the engagement ring.

Mavis and Kameo squealed and clapped at the news. Jax covered his ears with his hands. "Why do they do that?"

Gideon shook his head. "I'd say there's no fool like an old fool, but you'd kick my ass. Besides, I think Jordan is a catch."

Jax lined their party up and distributed the tickets, they did the obligatory photo with the Hula dancers and then headed to the top deck for music and a little dancing before dinner.

****

Brody pushed his plate back and folded his dinner napkin as he reached for his drink. "I've been filming off the island for a while, what else is new?"

Kameo grinned broadly. "Do you know Jax and Kirk are now co-partners in Silver SEAL Fitness?"

Brody nodded. "No kidding? Have I lost my script consultant?"

Jax touched his dinner napkin to his lips. "I'm not leading exercises or that stuff; it's on paper as an investment. I'm still your consultant. After reading that last script, I'd like to talk to you about some of my ideas."

206

"After we wrap this shoot, I'm taking a week on the island. My schedule is wide open because I need a holiday."

Kameo put a hand over Jax's. "When you're ready, why don't I make us dinner? You guys can talk big boom movies all night."

Flint waited while the server poured more wine and then leaned in closer. "Tell me about this act we're seeing, what does he do?"

Mavis nodded curiously. "I heard he worked in Vegas."

Gideon shrugged. "You met him; you know the stuff he divines. Remember the guy at Kirk's house?"

Kameo tsked and shook her head. "He's an intuitive and a medium. Without his warning, I might not be here now."

Jordon nodded. "He comes into the gym regularly; he's a sweet kid."

Kirk shifted in his chair and shook his head. "You say that about every young man who comes in and flirts with you."

"I like young men when they flirt with me, but who do I go home with?"

Kirk caught her hand and kissed it. "Some gnarly old bastard like me."

Jordan looked at the other guests at the table and winked. "I guess we could announce that I'm marrying this gnarly old bastard on Christmas Eve."

Kameo elbowed Jax. "You'd better get used to the excitement. Weddings are more fun than moving."

Jax nodded. "More cake samples, fewer furniture auctions."

The house lights blinked twice, and the announcer boomed, "Good evening to our guests, prepare to be amazed and astounded by the otherworldly revelations of Xavier, the Oracle."

The spotlight focused on a far more polished young performer than they'd seen in Vegas. His golden hair glinted

207

under the lights as his full lips pulled into a knowing smile. He winked at the table with his friends, bowed slightly, and then took the microphone in his hand.

"I'm drawn to this area of the room." He began at the table straight ahead of him. "Someone at this table has recently lost a mother figure." A young woman raised her hand. "This was not your mother who passed many years ago, but this person took her place in your life."

The young woman teared up. "My aunt raised me from the age of five."

Concentration showed on Des's face. "She makes me feel dizzy, and my head hurts."

The young woman nodded. "She had a stroke."

Des continued, "I feel it happened very quickly, you rushed her to the hospital, but there was nothing to be done."

The woman openly cried into her napkin. "That's right. She was already comatose by the time the ambulance arrived at the hospital."

Des put a comforting hand on her shoulder. "She wants you to know; she heard you say goodbye." Her face brightened, and she clasped Des's hand, nodding, and smiling. "She wants you to know she's grateful you gave her permission to leave and told her you'd be alright."

"That's true." The young woman gasped and stood.

Gideon looked around and whispered to the table. "Have you ever heard so much gobbledygook?" He shook his head and drained his Manhattan.

The audience applauded as she embraced Des. Des turned and headed directly to their table. He stopped in front of Gideon. "Yes, and no answers only, please. You understand?"

Gideon's mouth took on an unpleasant twist. "Yes."

"You are a lawman. But you're not completely satisfied with your work."

Gideon crossed his arms over his chest and shrugged.

"I'll take that as a yes." Gideon's friends at the table watched Des's complete concentration on Gideon to the point Gideon squirmed. "One of the reasons you're unhappy about your work is because it often takes you away from your son, who will have his eighth birthday in two weeks."

Gideon glared at Jax, who threw up his hands in surrender. "I've said nothing about anything."

"You've never been very good with people. You enjoy a solitary life, but you do regret losing the love of your boy's mother."

Gideon sat forward abruptly. Hands between his knees, hard eyes focused on Des. "If you don't take action to win her back within the next six months, the window will close, and your boy will have a new stepfather." He turned and placed gentle hands on Kirk and Jordan's shoulders. He stood for a moment; eyes closed. His lips moved silently, and he nodded. When his gaze widened at Kirk, his smile was resolute. "The holidays will see you celebrating a new union. Your marriage will be a true partnership. Your family has come through dark times, but that is behind you now. By this time next year, you'll be settled with all your children around you."

Des patted their shoulders and moved on to another table.

Kirk's gaze narrowed at the retreating figure and then stared at his friends at the table. Jordan giggled and waved him off. "I told you, the baby factory is closed."

Kameo raised a questioning hand. "He didn't say, grandchildren, did he?"

Jax levied a long look at his father. "How many liberty ports did you hit?"

A shadow of confusion crossed Kirk's face. "No more than you."

Jordan wrapped both hands around her lover's arm. "Something you want to tell me, dear?"

The End

Thank you for reading Roman's Rules. Stay in touch with us for the next chapter of their lives, Roman's Return Roman's Adventures, Book Three. (*Is Des correct?*)

If you enjoyed our story, the greatest gift you can give us is a simple review wherever you bought the book, at BookBub, GoodReads, or other book websites.

We look forward to meeting you at one of the many Author/Reader events listed on our Facebook page.

OTHER BOOKS BY AMBER ANTHONY

Roman's Revenge, Roman's Adventures, Book 1

Jax Roman is the image of courage, nobility, and strength. A clever mind and agile body propelled Roman to the head of his SEAL class.

Handsome and disarming, Jax is in charge of his world, vertical and horizontal. Now, at the pinnacle of his game, he leads his team until…the Lobos Cartel, the worst Jax has ever fought, sets out to eliminate him.

Lovely and compassionate, Dr. Kameo Alana meets Jax in his most desperate hour. Her family has borne the cartel's punishment.

Without Kameo, Jax would not be free to topple the depraved cartel. Kameo is more than a balm for his pain. Together they sizzle white-hot.

Jax's mission for a 'happily ever after' with Kameo is an exercise in 'taking no prisoners', SEAL style.

Arise, My Darling

Strangely gifted, Jacob King finds Cricket Nielson in his meditations between worlds. Delightful Cricket is a woman trapped first by injury and then her husband's villainy. Captivated by her buoyant spirit, intrigued by their elusive meetings, Jake uses his psychic talents to locate this imprisoned beauty.

Their meetings on the astral plane reveal they have loved each other for eons. This newly reignited love calls Jake to draw on every spiritual resource at his disposal. He convinces sympathetic law enforcement professionals to hear him out as he discovers a series of murders and knows Cricket is next.

Will the forces of the universe unite Jake and Cricket before the insidious serial killer strikes again?

Becoming Gabriel

Meet Gabriel Lee, if he were a young billionaire, his last few years would have earned him celebrity status. But, he's a mechanic in Baltimore's inner city. Past regrets haunt him. Can he ever win in a rigged system?

Opposites attract when Grace Lerner trades abusive privilege for freedom. Suddenly homeless, she meets Gabriel and in their unlikely bond, they find soulmates come from the darndest places.

When Gabriel's ghosts endanger their joy, criminals cause a painful separation. Will their devotion deliver their happily ever after?

Appetite for Blood, Prequel to the Blood Trilogy

A revolution is roaring into the 1920s! Vampires, who previously killed to feed, now thrill to feed.

The revolution is led by a four-hundred-year-old vampire, Rick Hiatt, and his newly turned ward, Matt Brenner.

This is not the first time Rick has encountered the brutal treachery of the Moreau family of vampires, but he and Matt seek to make it the last.

Los Angelinos mortal and immortal are under attack by the entitled, remorseless Moreaus. Dragon-shifter Adam Lachlan and seductresses Venus and Luna, team up with Rick and Matt to put an end to the siege.

Brute strength won't take these hellions down, but they might be hoodwinked into exposing themselves.

Read about the origins of the fast friendship between Matt, Rick, and Adam, and see how their BDSM empire grew from humble beginnings to an international conglomerate.

Blood Rising, Book One of the Blood Trilogy

Drop-dead gorgeous alive, Matt Brenner has never lacked for feminine attention. Undead, he's even more potent. Immortality would be stellar if only he accepted his life as a vampire. Matt and fellow vamp Richard Hiatt created a BDSM empire catering to Vampire/Doms and willing donor/subs who trade sexual ecstasy for blood. The clubs have made Matt's existence manageable, if uninspired.

Inspiration comes in the form of Catherine Temple.

Matt's made it a rule not to get emotionally involved with human women, and he sticks to it. Cat is the woman who can entice him to break all the rules. When Matt is introduced to a controversial drug that allows him a human lifetime with Cat, it's too exquisite to resist.

Powerful elements of the vampire nation are against it, and though Matt tries to protect Cat, love must be stronger than death.

Blood Emerald, Book Two of the Blood Trilogy

SDV (Single Dom Vampire) unknowingly ISO compassionate, sincere, spontaneous SMW (Single Mortal Woman). Extra points for patience, brains, and beauty. Handsome, powerful, Rick Hiatt has managed romance and sex within the roles of Dom/sub relationships for five hundred years. What if there is something more? What if the delicious Anna Curley, shielded from the world of dark sex games, can show him?

Rick returns to the helm of his international BDSM Empire after confronting a disaster within his vampire Family. His nemesis, Veronique

Moreau, could destroy the fragile veil between the Vamp/Mortal worlds, leaving vampires exposed. He meets Anna, a guileless young woman with enough savvy to see trouble coming in the form of a vampire hunter.

Their worlds collide. Swept into the dangers of preternatural conflict, Rick and Anna experience exquisite passion and heart-stopping peril. Is love enough? They could lose their lives as well as their hearts.

Blood Dragon, Book Three of the Blood Trilogy
Adam Lachlan, a tall drink of scrumptious masculinity, has been exiled from his dragon-shifter clan for the past two hundred years. His bad-boy charm has been harnessed to succeed as a Master Dom in the mortal world. He's spent decades isolating himself emotionally.

Willow Greer is beautiful, intelligent, and charming. Men have pursued her, but she's flown from them all. Willow has a secret burden. Adopted in infancy and having no explanation for shifting into a Pegasus at puberty, she's cloistered herself romantically. Without knowing the full truth of her nature, how can she commit to love?

When Adam's fire meets Willow's short fuse, flirtation is on! At the onset, secrets are guarded, but once their true selves are revealed, the complications begin. Can they overcome the problems of romance between different shifter species? Will they drop their emotional baggage and risk love's bondage?

WHERE TO FOLLOW AMBER ANTHONY

All Author
BookBub
BookSprout
Facebook Amber Anthony, Author
GoodReads
The Romance Reviews
Twitter @writeambera
Our website: https://www.AmberAnthonyWrites.com

DO YOU ENJOY TEA?
FIND US AT ADAGIO TEAS!

We have custom blended teas to correspond to each of our books. Purchasing these teas supports various charities Search under 'Blends', Keyword tagged Amber Anthony at Adagio.com. Each tea purchase benefits a charity with a 5% donation.

Joyfully, Jordan

Blended with Green Tea, Orange, Rose Hips, Hibiscus, Natural Orange Flavor, Marigold Flowers, Natural Mandarin Flavor, Natural Ginseng Flavor, and Ginger. Blood Orange, Mandarin Green, Ginseng Green. Accented with Orange Peels & Apricot

This tea supports the charity Random Acts, their mission is to conquer the world one random act of kindness at a time.

Kirk's Time-Out

Blended with Black Tea, Honeybush Tea, Cocoa Nibs, Natural Chocolate Flavor, Natural Hazelnut Flavor, and Natural Vanilla Flavor. Teas: Chocolate, Hazelnut, Honeybush Vanilla. Accented with Cocoa Nibs & Safflower. *This tea supports the Gary Sinise Foundation.*

www.ingramcontent.com/pod-product-compliance
Lightning Source LLC
Chambersburg PA
CBHW030740110726
47900CB00008B/2389